I REALLY CAN'T STAY

A. R. ROSE

Edited By: Virginia Tesi Carey

Proofread By: Amanda Bentley

Character Art & Back Cover Art by: @magrnarts

Zee

Chapter One

November twenty-ninth. Black Friday. The day after Thanksgiving. Otherwise known as hell to retail workers.

Looking out over the cash wrap, I watch as frenzied shoppers load their hand baskets with books and knick-knacks while holiday music blares through the store's speakers. The line to check out wraps and spans down the nearest aisle. Every check stand is manned, and my employees are situated around the store, helping customers find the perfect gifts for their loved ones. We're stocked, staffed, and operations are running smoothly, all things considered.

Still, it's the absolute worst time for my grief to hit me like a paperweight, socking me square in the stomach. Everything becomes muffled—my sight, my hearing. All I can recognize is the ringing in my ears.

Thanksgiving was hard. Christmas will be harder.

"Hey, Zee, are you okay?" one of the women on my staff asks. Her voice floats through the brain fog and pulls me back to reality. It's like someone has taken off my blindfold and unmuted the TV as the store comes rushing back into focus. "You look really pale. Do you need to sit down?"

"No, it's okay," I insist, shaking my head. I give her a tight-lipped smile and turn around to busy myself by straightening the go-backs that line the rear counter.

A tear trickles out from my bottom lashes and rolls down my cheek. Quickly, I swipe at it, erasing it from existence as I bite my lip to keep more from falling.

For a second, I allow myself to close my eyes as I grip the counter tightly, counting backward in my head while inhaling and exhaling as I attempt to ground myself.

Four...

Three...

"Hey, Zee! Can I get a price override?" another employee calls out from a few registers down.

My eyes snap open, and I turn around with a grin in place. "On my way!" I singsong as I hurry over to where he stands with an annoyed looking customer.

The next three hours fly by, and when I'm finally able to collapse on the break room couch, I barely muster the energy to pull my homemade PB&J out of my lunch bag. Settling back against the cushions, I close my eyes.

Someone entering the room quickly disturbs my peace, though, so I go back to the sandwich I'm holding and peel back the foil it's wrapped in.

"Hey, Zee! Hope I'm not bugging you," my friend

Genesis apologizes as she starts rustling around her locker.

"You're not." I take a small bite of my sandwich. "I like your claw-clip." Her black curly hair is pulled back with a red oversized clip with vintage looking Christmas lights that are lit up.

Genesis lives a few floors up in my building, and we met one afternoon as we were both waiting for the elevator. She started here a few weeks ago as a seasonal employee to make a few extra bucks while she's going through nursing school. We've grown closer recently, and it's nice to have someone to call a friend, even though I've been selective about the things I've told her.

She smiles. "Thanks! I just got it a couple of days ago. My mom, sisters, and I all bought matching ones to wear on Christmas, but it's too cute to not wear more than that."

My face falls at the mention of her family, and I must not be quick enough to correct it because her eyes widen and she immediately apologizes again.

"Ah, so you've heard." *Word travels quickly around here.* "It's fine, Gen. Never be sorry for speaking about your family."

It's not your fault I don't have one anymore.

"I know we haven't exactly reached this level in our friendship yet, but if you need a place to spend the holidays, my family would be happy to have you over. We have a huge family and it's a 'the more the merrier' type of vibe for us."

"That's sweet, but I'll be fine."

"What'd you do for Thanksgiving?"

Sat on my couch watching reruns of Gossip Girl while eating a rotisserie chicken and cranberries from a can. "I kept it low-key."

Genesis assesses me silently while taking a bite of her own sandwich—turkey with cheese. She purses her lips, then stands abruptly. "I'm gonna go to the cafe and grab a coffee. You want one?"

Finishing my sandwich, I crumple the foil and toss it into the trash can just a few feet away. "No thanks, I'll never sleep tonight if I have one now."

"I wish I had that problem! I sleep like the dead." Genesis flinches. "Shit! I'm so sorry."

I laugh, but it's the fake laugh I've had ever since I became numb. "It's okay," I reassure her. "Don't worry about it."

Before she leaves the room, she stops and says, "There's still a whole month. If you change your mind about coming, let me know. No one should be alone on Christmas."

Don't I know it, but what's a girl to do when the only family I had died over the summer?

My dogs are barking.

Not in the literal sense—I don't own a dog, just a tubby

brown cat named Potato. My feet ache like I've been walking on shards of glass all day.

After pulling two hours of overtime, the only thing I want is a glass of white wine and a scalding hot bubble bath with some Epsom salts, and the candy cane bath bomb I've been excited to use.

As the water runs, I heat a slice of leftover pizza in the microwave and pour the rest of an open wine bottle into my glass, taking a large gulp of it once the final drop has landed. With a minute left, I head to my room and shimmy out of my work clothes, tossing them into the laundry basket before walking back into the kitchen naked as the day I was born to retrieve my slice of greasy heaven.

Potato meows at me as he circles my feet, rubbing against my ankles. He's trying to butter me up so he can have a second helping of dinner, but the little beast needs to go on a diet per his veterinarian's instructions.

The pizza's piping hot as I pull it from the microwave and tip my head back to take a bite. Of course, it burns my tongue, but I eat it anyway, and grab my glass of wine. Potato follows me into the bathroom and watches me as I sink into the bathwater that shimmers with a pink hue from the bath bomb. The water curls around me like a hug and I take another bite of the pizza, sad that it's almost gone already.

Shutting the water off with my foot, Potato takes that as his invitation to jump onto the edge. He nearly falls in, freaked out by the water that sloshed onto where his foot is now, but he rights himself and situates his fluffy butt into a comfortable position.

Laughing, I shake my head at my feline companion. "Potato, you're a hot mess."

His judgy eyes track my movements as I take another large gulp of my wine.

The hot water is slowly releasing the tension from my body, so I sink deeper, letting it come up to my chin. Loose tendrils of my blonde hair that have escaped from my clip are getting wet, but I can't bring myself to care. Right now, I'm in my happy place. It's the only time I feel any sense of contentment, and the only time I feel like I can think and let my mind wander into whatever direction it wants to go.

Evidently, my mind wants to recite my friend's words on replay because I can't stop thinking *"No one should be alone on Christmas,"* in my mind.

And you know what? She's right. No one should be alone on any holiday, *especially* Christmas.

I don't know how I'm going to survive it alone.

For as long as I can remember, it's always only been Mom and Dad, me, and Miles, living in sunny San Diego.

Now there's just me.

No one should be alone on Christmas.

Making a rash decision, I jolt upward, sloshing more water from the tub and soaking Potato's underside. He meows with vexation before jumping down and sprinting from the room, his belly swinging in full glory as I laugh and reach for my phone on the bathroom counter.

Is this the dumbest thing I've ever done? Possibly. But I'm going to do it, anyway.

My fingers fly across the screen as I look for the SparksFly app I downloaded last month but never followed through with. I got as far as uploading a profile photo before chickening out.

The little blue icon taunts me as I stare at it, my thumb hovering, but not clicking it...until I do.

I'm a full on cliché when I release the breath I didn't know I was holding and am prompted to complete my profile.

Bio.

Clicking it, I don't think about what I type, I just do it.

THERE'S FOUR WEEKENDS LEFT BEFORE CHRISTMAS, AND NO ONE SHOULD HAVE TO SHOW UP TO THEIR HOLIDAY PARTIES ALONE. NEED A DATE? SOMEONE TO BRING TO YOUR OFFICE PARTY SO YOUR FRENEMY STOPS GIVING YOU GRIEF ABOUT YOUR LACK OF A SPOUSE? OR TO YOUR FAMILY DINNER SO YOUR PARENTS STOP BREATHING DOWN YOUR NECK ABOUT SETTLING DOWN?

NO STRINGS ATTACHED. NO SEX. JUST A HOLIDAY PARTY DATE. A HOLIDATE, IF YOU WILL.

Going back to the section for my name, I delete Elizabeth Ashford and stare at the empty box for what feels like eternity.

Maybe this is a stupid idea.

Then it hits me. A name comes to me like a whisper in my mind.

Holly North, I type. My lips curl into a smile at the perfect little Christmas persona I've just created in ten letters.

Before I let fear freeze me, I hit *submit*, and the screen changes to the main dashboard of my app, showing me four very attractive men it thinks I'd match with.

Instead of perusing, I lock my home screen and toss my phone onto the carpet below the tub.

There. I did it.

But what exactly did I do?

Zee

Chapter Two

Bright sunlight streams in through the sheer curtains I thought would be cute, but instead are proving to be the worst idea ever, waking me from a restless sleep.

I tossed and turned all night, and if this headache is any indication, then today's going to suck.

On the pillow next to me, Potato purrs, still sound asleep and looking as comfy as can be. Bouncing my hand against the bed, I feel for where I put my phone until I find it, and bring it to eye level. Twelve notifications wait for me from the SparksFly app, and I groan, remembering what I did last night.

Damn the effects of hot water and wine, making me do stupid things because bath time Zee thinks her ideas are so great, then *future* Zee has to clean up the messes later.

Coffee.

I desperately need a cup of coffee before I see what's happening on the app. There's a lump in my throat as I crawl out of bed and shove my feet inside of my platform Ugg slippers.

Padding into the kitchen, I turn on the single-cup coffee maker. It grumbles and groans as the water heats up, and I busy myself grabbing a mug, and peppermint mocha creamer.

The urge to read the notifications becomes too much to wait for the coffee maker to finish, and I unlock my phone. The app immediately pops up and brings me to my dashboard. Five matches and six messages await me. I start with the matches first.

Thomas, twenty-eight, San Diego. Padres fan, season ticket holder. Has a golden retriever named Tobias and loves to spend his weekends exploring hiking trails around the city. He's cute. The golden retriever seems accurate—he looks like he'd own one.

Next up is Rhett, twenty-four, La Jolla. He's an aspiring musician, loves late nights listening to the waves at the beach, and has plans to move to LA in the spring.

He lives in La Jolla, which tells me everything I need to know—he still lives with his parents.

Cole seems promising, though, with his bright hazel eyes and lopsided smile. He's thirty, says he loves to read, and works for the state of California.

Oh...wait, no. He lives in Santee. Pass.

The last guy I've matched with, I barely glance at before I toggle over to the messages. Before I tackle those, though, I pour my coffee and gently stir in my creamer before I head to the couch. My buffalo plaid blanket awaits, and as I kick off my slippers and curl into my favorite corner, I turn on a Christmas movie for some background noise.

Pulling my attention back to my phone, I start with the first message that was sent.

Message received

SUBJECT: TOO FORWARD?

YOU'RE ABSOLUTELY GORGEOUS, HOLLY. I'D LOVE TO BRING YOU TO MY OFFICE CHRISTMAS PARTY ON THE THIRTEENTH. THE COMPANY RENTED OUT A BACKROOM AT A RESTAURANT IN THE GASLAMP DISTRICT. LET ME KNOW IF YOU'RE AVAILABLE, AND I'D BE HAPPY TO SEND YOU SOME MONEY TO SHOP FOR AN OUTFIT AND PROVIDE MORE DETAILS.

XX,
ETHAN HANSON

———

Clicking on Ethan's profile, a smile forms when I see he's not a complete troll. He's my age, twenty-eight, and a software engineer.

Why's he single?

Probably the same reason I am. People suck.

The next message I click on is in the middle of the list, but the subject is intriguing.

Message received

SUBJECT: NOT A PARTY

NOT A PARTY, BUT I FOUND A TWO-FOR-ONE DEAL ON A COOKIE DECORATING EVENT IN LIBERTY STATION FOR DECEMBER EIGHTH. YOU IN?

MATEO REYES

———

Laughing into my coffee, I roll my eyes playfully even though *Mateo* can't see it, then toggle to the next message.

Message received

SUBJECT: HOLIDAY SOS

HOLLY? IT'S ME, AXEL. I'M BEING FORCED TO ATTEND MY FAMILY'S ANNUAL UGLY SWEATER-THEMED PIE BAKING COMPETITION AND PRE-CHRISTMAS DINNER. WOULD YOU—AND I ASK THIS ON MY KNEES BEGGING AT YOUR FEET— PLEASE GO SHOPPING WITH ME TO FIND THE UGLIEST MATCHING SWEATERS WE CAN FIND AND GO WITH ME TO WHAT IS SURE TO BE THE BIGGEST SHITSHOW THAT WILL HAUNT YOUR HOLIDAYS UNTIL THE END OF TIME?

WHAT'S A GUY GOTTA DO FOR YOU TO SAY YES?

I'LL GROVEL. I'M PRETTY GOOD AT IT.

SIGNED,
YOUR FAVORITE STRANGER EVER, AXEL HARRIS

———

Axel seems fun, although I have to say, I'm not a fan of his name. That's not really a prerequisite or anything, though. I'm just doing this to pass the time and not be alone for the entire holiday season. Taking another drink of my coffee, I'm about to go into the next message when a brand new one pops up, so I click it instead.

Message received

SUBJECT: QUICK QUESTION: ANGEL OR STAR

WHICH GOES ON TOP OF THE CHRISTMAS
TREE?

-TRISTIAN

———

There's a little green dot by his profile picture, indicating that he's still online. When I visit his profile, the image of a man in a backward hat wearing a huge smile on his face as he stands in front of a lake greets me. He's cute in that All-American boy sort of way.

Going back to the message, I reply.

SUBJECT: QUICK QUESTION: ANGEL
OR STAR

ANGEL.

-HOLLY

———

Message received

SUBJECT: QUICK QUESTION: ANGEL
OR STAR

RIGHT ANSWER. NEXT QUESTION.

PRESENTS OPENED ON CHRISTMAS EVE OR
CHRISTMAS MORNING?

-TRISTIAN

———

SUBJECT: QUICK QUESTION: ANGEL
OR STAR

MORNING. YOU?

-HOLLY

———

Message received

SUBJECT: QUICK QUESTION: ANGEL
OR STAR

I'M THE ONE ASKING THE QUESTIONS, MS.
NORTH.

EGGNOG OR APPLE CIDER?

-T

————

SUBJECT: QUICK QUESTION: ANGEL
OR STAR

OOH, THAT WOULD DEPEND ON THE
OCCASION.

CIDER WITH DINNER. EGGNOG WHILE
SITTING IN FRONT OF THE FIREPLACE WITH
A BOOK.

-HOLLY

————

Smiling into my coffee again, I feel optimistic for the first time in weeks. Who knew all I needed was a little rapid-fire holiday questions sesh over a dating app?

Message received

SUBJECT: QUICK QUESTION: ANGEL
OR STAR

YOU'RE BEING TIED UP. IS IT WITH TINSEL
OR CHRISTMAS LIGHTS?

-T

————

And...this is where he loses me. My heart plummets into my stomach, immediately uncomfortable with the question. It's clear to see it has a double meaning, and it makes me shift in my seat. Do I reply? Ignore it? What's the protocol here?

It feels like I'm moving in slow motion as I click the reply button and type my message, deleting it several times before I finally hit send. Nothing I say will be adequate to what I am feeling, but maybe he didn't mean it in a weird way?

Of course he did. Either way he meant it would be weird.

SUBJECT: QUICK QUESTION: ANGEL OR STAR

...WHAT?

-HOLLY

———

My heart hammers in my chest as I wait for him to respond, and to his nature, or so I've gathered in this short interaction, his reply is nearly immediate.

Message Received

SUBJECT: QUICK QUESTION: ANGEL OR STAR

IF I WERE TO TIE YOU UP, WOULD YOU PREFER TO BE TIED WITH TINSEL OR CHRISTMAS LIGHTS? I SAW CHRISTMAS LIGHTS BEING DONE IN A BOOK ONCE AND IT SEEMED LIKE FUN. THE GUY DIDN'T PLUG THEM IN, BUT WE COULD TRY THAT, IF YOU WERE DOWN.

-T

———

The moment my eyes drag over the closing of his message, I click on his profile and hit the bright red block button that sits at the bottom.

Goodbye Tristian from San Marcos. Please don't ever try to find me again.

A shiver runs through me with disgust, and I take a gulp of my coffee, letting it warm my insides. That seems like enough messages for the day, but I still have several I haven't read yet. Honestly, they can wait. Later, I'll reply to Mateo, and I'll say yes to the party with Ethan and Axel, too. Axel's pie sweater party thing actually sounds really fun.

Tossing my phone onto the couch, I sink further into the cushions and turn the volume up on the TV so I can watch the movie I put on. I have a few hours before I need to be at work, so I might as well make the best of the quiet solitude before I make my way back into the holiday shopping craze.

"Hey, boss! What are you doing here on a Saturday?" Genesis asks as I slip into the break room to put my purse in my locker.

"Covering for Peter." The metal scrapes against itself, clashing with my words. "He went out of town for Thanksgiving and doesn't come back until tomorrow."

"Oh, that's nice of you," she muses as I engage my lock. Giving her a smile, I pass her on my way to the door. Telling her I'm taking her advice and making plans not to be alone this holiday season is on the tip of my tongue, but I'm not sure how much information I want to share with her.

"See you out there," I say instead and head onto the main floor. My shoulder clips the wall on my way out, and I hiss, bringing my hand to rub the tender spot.

The bookstore is bustling with people shopping, which is amazing to see. Thanks to the uptick in social media influencers talking about books on various platforms, independent bookstores are flourishing. A fresh shipment of books should be here on Monday, and I was excited to see one of the indie authors I just took a chance on ordering went viral. We've already had three calls asking if we have her book in stores.

The timing is perfect.

By the end of my shift, my legs and feet ache. I wore my most comfortable pair of combat boots—the heel's only two inches—but it seems like this is my body's way of telling me I'm getting too old to prioritize cute over comfort.

In my defense, they were the cutest pair of shoes to pair with my black sweater, buffalo plaid skirt, and black tights.

The cafe is quiet tonight, so I decide to grab myself a tea before leaving, and as I check my phone while I wait, my breath hitches at the number of notifications waiting for me from SparksFly.

How can I have thirty-two messages?

Scrolling through the insane amount of messages, I'm too overwhelmed to open any of them.

How can this many people need a date for a holiday gathering?

There's one message that catches my eye as I'm about to close out of the app, so I open it while I wait for my tea.

Message received

SUBJECT: HOW MANY MESSAGES HAVE
YOU RECEIVED?

I'M PLACING BETS ON AT LEAST TWENTY
BY NOW.
HI. MY NAME IS LINCOLN. I'M THIRTY YEARS
OLD AND LIVE IN MIRA MESA. YOUR BIO
WAS INTRIGUING TO ME–IT WAS AS
THOUGH YOU HEARD MY INNER THOUGHTS
AND PUT THEM INTO A SENTENCE. YES, MY
FAMILY IS BREATHING DOWN MY NECK TO
SETTLE DOWN. AS A DOCTOR, I DON'T HAVE
A LOT OF TIME TO SOCIALIZE, LET ALONE
MEET SOMEONE WHO ISN'T A COLLEAGUE.
MY PARENTS ARE INSISTING I COME FOR
DINNER ON CHRISTMAS EVE SINCE I'M
SCHEDULED TO BE AT THE HOSPITAL IN
THE AFTERNOON ON CHRISTMAS. I'D LOVE
TO HAVE SOMEONE BY MY SIDE SO THE
MEAL (AND THE HOLIDAY) IS ENJOYABLE
AND NOT PEPPERED WITH QUESTIONS
ABOUT WHEN I'M GOING TO FIND A
SPECIAL SOMEONE.
I KNOW ASKING FOR YOUR TIME ON
CHRISTMAS EVE IS A STRETCH, BUT I
FIGURED IT WOULDN'T HURT TO TRY.

LOOKING FORWARD TO HEARING BACK.

LINCOLN STOKES

For whatever reason, a smile forms on my lips as I read the message from Lincoln. When I'm done, my eyes drift to his profile bubble and I see the green dot. My heart rate quickens, remembering the conversation with the last guy, and I hesitate.

I decided to do this for a reason, I remind myself, swallowing thickly.

No one should have to be alone on Christmas, Genesis' voice echoes through my mind.

> SUBJECT: HOW MANY MESSAGES HAVE
> YOU RECEIVED?
>
> A DECENT AMOUNT. SEEMS THERE ARE A
> LOT OF SAN DIEGANS WHO NEED SUPPORT
> AROUND THE HOLIDAYS. CHRISTMAS EVE
> SOUNDS GREAT. I DON'T HAVE ANYTHING
> PLANNED AS OF NOW.
>
> -HOLLY
>
> —

Clenching my jaw, I reread the message and feel a little remorseful at the undertone I gave it. It was a bit short... cold, almost.

"Zee?" the cafe's barista calls from behind the counter as she places my tea in the pickup area.

Picking it up, I tell her thank you even though her back is already to me as she makes another beverage. The app's notification signals, pulling my attention back to the device in my hand.

Eagerly, I open it and read.

Message received

> SUBJECT: HOW MANY MESSAGES HAVE
> YOU RECEIVED?
>
> DO YOU MIND A BIT OF TRAVEL? MY
> PARENTS LIVE IN JULIAN.
>
> LINCOLN STOKES
>
> —

Stowing my phone in my purse, I leave Lincoln's message unanswered and focus on my surroundings as I walk to my car. Holding my longest key between my knuckles, I scan the parking lot and wait until I'm standing next to my beat-up Subaru Forester to unlock it. Familiarity comforts me as I sink into the driver's seat and lock the doors, breathing in the vanilla-suede scent of my air freshener.

It takes fifteen minutes and two freeways to get home, and another five before I'm inside, stripping away my clothes as the water for the shower warms.

Bobby pin after bobby pin, the tightness on my scalp begins to dissipate as I remove the pins and ties from my hair. Shoving my fingers into the blonde locks, I rub at my scalp, loosening it further. It feels like heaven—almost as good as it feels to take off your bra at the end of a long shift.

The water is scalding as I enter the small shower-tub combo and pull the curtain closed. Steam rises around me while I take my time washing the day away.

My thoughts drift to the messages I've received, the amount of responses surprising me all over again.

When I emerge from the shower, Potato is sitting on the sink waiting for me. Instinctually, I reach to pet him, and he immediately jumps from the counter and races away as water droplets fall from my skin. I think he's still mad about his near-drowning experience yesterday. You know, the one where he didn't actually fall into the water but acted like he had?

As I dress, the soft, buttery fabric of my favorite Christmas jammies curls around my skin like a warm hug. They're cozy, as are my slippers as I push my feet into them and head to the couch. My tea is lukewarm by the time I pick it up again and sip it, but it's almost gone, so I keep it in my grasp while searching for a feel-good movie on TV.

Three more notifications from the SparksFly app come through before I settle on *Elf*, an oldie but goodie, and force myself to watch a few minutes of the movie before I read through the messages.

More of the same, I think as I float over the words these new men have sent me.

Office party.

Family dinner.

...a funeral?

That last one is an absolute 'hell no' from me.

Then there's Lincoln's message, the one I feel bad about not yet answering. He seems like a good guy, if the eloquence in his message was anything to judge by. He's a doctor—that's an honorable profession. And he was honest and upfront about why he needed my help.

Julian is a bit of a drive, about an hour, but it's not out of the question. Christmas Eve is slated to be spent alone and on my couch anyway, probably with some Vietnamese takeout or something. Why not spend it with this guy and his family? Plus Julian is beautiful, and at Christmastime I bet the small town does something special. I wouldn't mind getting some of their famous pies too...

Okay—yeah, why not?

Christmas Eve in Julian with the Stokes family.

SUBJECT: HOW MANY MESSAGES HAVE
YOU RECEIVED?

JULIAN ISN'T THAT FAR 🙂

COUNT ME IN. LET ME KNOW THE DETAILS
WHEN YOU HAVE THEM.

-HOLLY

———

Zee

Chapter Three

Message received

SUBJECT: NOT A PARTY

I CAN'T WAIT TO FIND OUT WHICH OF US IS
THE BETTER COOKIE DECORATOR. SEE YOU
TONIGHT.

MATEO REYES

—

Light raindrops scatter against the windshield of my car, the sound mingling with the soft *click-click click-click* of my turn signal as I turn from Rosecrans Street and into the area of San Diego known as Liberty Station. The old Navy training center has become a popular spot to hang out, shop, and eat, and is situated on hundreds of acres of businesses, parks, and venues. It's gorgeous—one of my favorite places to visit.

In theory, I should be more excited than I am to be

here, but the nerves have taken over. The reality that I'm about to meet a stranger has settled in.

Pulling into a parking spot, I turn off the car and look out toward the small strip of water that separates Liberty Station from the airport. The marine layer is thick, and I shiver preemptively, already knowing I'm going to be cold the second I turn my car off and exit its warmth.

I've parked a little far from where Mateo and I are meeting up, but it's busy tonight, and parking was hard to find.

We're meeting inside Public Market to grab a coffee before we decorate cookies, and I question whether agreeing to this date was a good idea since it goes against the entire point of why I'm doing this.

I'm not looking to date someone. Ever since my family died, that part of me shut off—my love just...disappeared. Think Stefan Salvatore in *The Vampire Diaries* turning off his humanity. That's me, just with love.

I've accepted it, and it's the exact reason I'm seeking no-strings-attached companionship this holiday season. I just want to be someone's date to an event they don't want to show up alone to, but for whatever reason, I was compelled to say yes to meeting Mateo.

To rip off the Band-Aid, so to speak.

You've got this, I give myself a pep talk as I white-knuckle the door handle. Closing my eyes, I try to envision the date and how it will play out, hoping that I'm right.

As soon as I push the car door open, the thick, chilly air kisses my nose and cheeks, sending a shiver through me. While walking away from my car, I click the key fob to lock it no less than six times for extra lockiness, then once more for good measure, but I end up being too far.

The closer I get to Public Market, the upscale food court that Liberty Station is known for, the more intensely my heart starts hammering in my chest. Standing just outside one of the entrances is a man looking almost as nervous as I am as he bounces on the balls of his feet. He's wearing a navy blue puffer jacket—but it's one of the thin ones, not the ultra puffy ones like I prefer for myself—and dark wash jeans, with his hands stuffed into the pockets of his pants. His hair is dark and styled, and I'm surprised to see he's wearing glasses.

They look good on him. Really, really, good.

Scanning the parking lot again, his eyes meet mine as I emerge from between the two cars I momentarily hid behind so I could scope him out.

"Holly? Hi!" he calls out as I draw closer, and my smile widens. He's giving off good energy—kind energy. Not 'I'm actually a creepy stalker serial killer who wants to wear your flesh' kind of energy.

"Hey, so nice to—" But my sentence is cut short as I trip on the curb, stumbling and almost falling, before I'm able to get my balance back. Unfortunately for my pride, Mateo somehow is able to close the distance to me and try to catch me. As he bends, I stand, and my head collides with his jaw.

"Ow!"

"Shit!"

Cradling his chin, Mateo scrunches his eyes together, clearly in pain. "Well, that's one way to introduce yourself. Are you okay?"

Mortified, I take a step back and cross my arms over my chest. "I'm so sorry, Mateo. I can leave, I should go—"

"No, stop," he takes a step forward, "don't be silly. We have cookies waiting for us, remember?"

"Are you sure? I'm pretty sure I just assaulted you."

"Nah, I'm the one who wanted to be a white knight and save the damsel from her impending doom of a scraped knee. That collision was my bad."

His lopsided smile makes me smile, and a warm fuzzy haze sweeps through me as he extends his hand for me to take. "Come on, we need something warm to drink before we consume our body weight in cookies and frosting."

"Just our body weight?" I ask, taking his hand. The gesture is friendly, and although I feel a little crazy for immediately holding hands with a stranger, it doesn't feel awkward or weird.

He laughs. "Ah, I've got a sweet tooth on my hands, do I?"

"Maybe just a little."

Stopping in front of the coffee counter, I scan the menu and figure out what I want to drink, settling on peppermint tea. Coffee sounds better, but even with decaf, I'll be up all night if I drink it past two o'clock. Mateo orders our drinks, and I find us a table nearby to sit at until the cookie decorating begins.

"So tell me about yourself, Holly North," he says as he

takes the seat across from me a few minutes later, passing me my tea.

"What do you want to know?" I'm horrible at talking about myself. Give me a direct question and I can answer just fine. Ask me to just dive in and start telling you things about my life, and I freeze.

"How long have you lived in San Diego?"

"Pretty much my entire life. You?"

"Just moved here for work about three months ago. Hence, finding a stranger to decorate cookies with me."

"Is cookie decorating your thing?"

"Nah, I just thought it sounded like something cutesy to do for the holidays with a pretty lady."

"Ah, so what came first, finding the deal on the cookies or finding the lady?"

His eyes narrow playfully as he takes a long sip of his drink, then he laughs. "A gentleman can't tell all his secrets."

We fall into a playful banter for the rest of the time we sit and relax until we can go decorate our sweet treats. Set up as a pop-up style venue, we're greeted by three rows of tables adorned with every type of sugar cookie cut-out shape, frosting color, and type of sprinkle you can think of. Immediately, I feel giddy, and don't hesitate before pulling Mateo through the doors to find a space and wait for further instruction.

Showing our proof of payment to the woman who comes to greet us, she explains the rules and hands us both thin fabric aprons.

"They're really quite simple. Wash your hands prior to touching the cookies and always use the utensils for the application of the frosting and sprinkles. Absolutely no licking your hands if you get frosting on them, and if you choose to eat your cookies while you're here rather than take them home, please feel free to sit at one of the tables along the side. You each get a half dozen cookies to select and decorate. If you need me, my name is Sandra."

"Thank you, Sandra," I tell the woman sweetly, then look back at Mateo.

"Don't lick the frosting off our hands if it gets on them? Uh. Way to ruin the fun," he whispers, and I burst out laughing.

Stepping closer to the cookie table, I take in all of my options.

"Are any of them speaking to you?" Mateo reaches for a reindeer. "This one spoke to me. He said, pick me, you ho ho ho."

Once again, I can't control the laughter that bubbles out of me. "I think I want one of these." Grabbing a snowman, I purse my lips, then reach for a present. "And maybe this one."

Mateo picks up a mitten, sled, Santa head, elf, and gingerbread man, while I pick up a candy cane, Christmas tree, sweater, and star. There are red and green boxes at the end of the table to lay the cookies in, so we grab those, too, before going to the frosting table.

Time flies by as we live in the moment while playing with our sugary treats, laughing uncontrollably, and singing painfully off-key along with the carols that play through the sound system. Two hours and twelve horrific-looking cookies later, we finish, both covered in frosting. I'm pretty sure there's even a glob of it on my eyelash.

"Can I walk you to your car?" Mateo asks as we leave, walking in the direction I arrived in.

"Yeah." I smile at him and look down at the box in my hand before gazing forward. The parking lot has thinned, and I can see my car in the distance.

Nerves trickle their way back into my system because I know we've reached that point in the evening where we'll arrive at a crossroads, and I'll have a decision to make.

My stomach dips in anticipation when we come to a stop in front of my car and Mateo takes the box from my hands so I can fish my keys out of my purse. Unlocking it, I watch him open the back driver's door and place the cookies on the floorboard before shutting them inside.

"I had a great time tonight," I tell him earnestly. "Thank you for asking me to come with you."

"This is the most fun I've had since I moved here. I haven't laughed that hard since I was in college."

I can't remember the last time I laughed that hard, period.

Placing his box of cookies on top of my car, he steps closer and weaves his hand through my hair, resting it on the back of my neck. His fingers are cold against my skin as he draws me in, and I swallow thickly, wondering if I even really want to kiss him.

When his lips press against mine, butterflies stir in my

stomach, taking flight in a slow, melodic way. Mateo kisses with experience, deepening it in a way that's respectful, yet tells me without words exactly what he's interested in.

And as much as I enjoyed his company tonight, I'm just not looking for anything further than what we've already shared.

I shouldn't have let him kiss me.

Breaking the kiss, I lick my lips as our gaze meets, and a dopey smile settles on his face.

"Mateo, I really can't—"

"Shh," he whispers, kissing me again softly. "No strings, no sex," he recites my SparksFly bio. Reaching for the box sitting on my car, he takes it, then buries one hand in his pocket. "I'll see you around, Holly North. Get home safe."

Dumbfounded, I watch as he walks backward away from me. "That's it then?" I call out to him, equal parts happy and confused.

He shrugs and repeats, "Get home safe, Holly," still walking backward.

Realizing he won't turn around until I'm in my car, I shake my head and laugh before slipping into the driver's seat. Touching my fingers to my lips, I smile again, feeling like Mateo actually healed something inside me tonight. The date went great, and even though I'm not delusional enough to think they will all go off without a hitch, I can honestly say I'm excited to see what the others bring.

I'm excited for more laughter. More fun. More *warmth*.

I can do this.

Three more weeks. Three more dates.

Maybe this holiday season won't be as lonely as I thought.

Chapter Four

Message received

SUBJECT: TOO FORWARD?

THANKS AGAIN FOR BEING MY DATE TONIGHT. I'M LOOKING FORWARD TO MEETING YOU. I'LL WAIT FOR YOU IN FRONT OF CAFÈ 101, AND WE'LL GO IN TOGETHER.

SOME THINGS YOU SHOULD KNOW BEFORE MEETING UP WITH ME, IN CASE MY COWORKERS BRING IT UP (OUR COMPANY ISN'T HUGE AND EVERYONE KNOWS FAR TOO MUCH ABOUT EACH OTHER).

1. I DESPISE ONIONS.
2. I HAVE A SCAR THROUGH MY LEFT
EYEBROW FROM A BMX BIKING ACCIDENT
THREE YEARS AGO. SOMETIMES YOU
TRULY CANNOT, IN FACT, TEACH AN OLD
DOG NEW TRICKS.
3. I'M THE OLDEST OF SIX. WE GREW UP
HERE IN SAN DIEGO, BUT I'M THE ONLY ONE
WHO STILL LIVES HERE.
4. MY FAVORITE COLOR IS BURNT ORANGE.
5. I HAVE A GERMAN SHEPHERD NAMED
OTIS, AND A CAT NAMED CALLIE.

I'M NOT SURE WHY I FEEL THESE ARE
IMPORTANT THINGS YOU SHOULD KNOW,
BUT THERE YOU HAVE IT.

SEE YOU LATER,
ETHAN HANSON

———

The lights of downtown San Diego glitter against the fog that's sweeping through the city, shining brightly against the white haze. Rubbing my sweaty palms against my red velvet dress, I blow out a shaky breath and get myself into character. Ethan had sent me some basic facts about himself—things someone who's actually dating him would know—but for some reason, I don't think I'm going to need to know any of it.

Nerves zip through my system as the rideshare driver approaches the restaurant, pulling over in the loading zone.

"Thank you so much," I tell the woman as my fingers dance across my phone screen to leave her a tip on the app.

"Of course, hunny. Have a great time."

Slipping out of the car, my black strappy heels touch the asphalt, and I wrap my shawl around my shoulders. As I make my way behind the vehicle, the driver leaves, and at that exact moment, my eyes meet with a man who is clearly Ethan.

His smile radiates hotter than the sun. He's beautiful in person—like a Greek God. His blue eyes are piercing, glowing brightly in contrast to the navy blue suit he's wearing. The lack of tie and a couple of unbuttoned buttons are really doing it for me.

"Hi," he greets as I approach, taking me in. His eyes rake over my body, and for a moment, butterflies stir in my stomach.

Why did I come up with a no sex rule again?

"Ethan, hi," I say with more confidence than I'm feeling. Extending my hand, we shake, and he pulls me into his arms in a tight hug. I'm a little thrown off by the gesture, and stiffen in his arms.

"This is so weird, but also strangely exhilarating."

"I know. So what should I expect?"

Taking a step back, he rubs his hands down my arms. "Hor d'oeuvres, drinks, maybe some dancing, and a bunch of tech geeks. HR rented out the back room of this place," he gestures at the restaurant behind us, "and instead of having a sit-down dinner, they decided to treat it like more of a small-scale party."

"That sounds like fun. Not as much pressure to maintain conversation, either," I point out.

Ethan's eyes sparkle with amusement. "I hope you plan to converse with me, at least."

"Of course!" My cheeks heat with embarrassment as I replay what I just said in my mind. "I didn't mean I don't want to talk to *you*, just that there's less room for error with everyone else!"

"I know what you meant, Holly. Don't worry." He smiles again as I visibly relax. "So, how long have we been dating?"

"You tell me."

"Well, everyone was surprised I was bringing a date. I said it was new. So, maybe a month? Couple weeks?"

My lips purse in thought, and I don't miss the way Ethan's eyes lower to look at them. "A couple weeks is good. That way, if I get caught not knowing something about you, it's not as suspicious."

"Sounds great. Thanks again, Holly. I appreciate you doing this."

"No one should have to face the holidays alone."

For a second, I stop and think about why a man this attractive has to have a stand-in date, but I shake the thought away. It's none of my business.

"You're right." He wraps his arm around my shoulders. "No one should."

As he pulls open the door, the noise of the restaurant overtakes the quiet sounds from the street. Ethan stops to talk to the hostess, and she leads us to the back, where the holiday party is being held.

The second the French doors open, the entire crowd

erupts in excitement with a collective round of "Ay!" for Ethan's arrival. It's infectious, and my smile widens as I watch him shake hands with his coworkers and say hello to their spouses.

Pushing a lock of hair behind my ear, I stand behind him, not really sure how to act. It only takes a second before Ethan begins introducing me as his girlfriend.

"Oh, girly pop, you don't know what you've gotten yourself into with this one here," a petite blonde woman drawls, her southern accent thick as she backward jabs her thumb in Ethan's direction. "Stubborn as a mule, this one."

"All work and no play makes Ethan a dull boy, isn't that right, Bossman?"

Bossman?

"I'm not your boss, Randal," Ethan volleys back at him in a bored tone. He rolls his eyes dramatically at me, making me laugh.

"You sure think you are! Bossy as hell when we're on a deadline."

"It's called leadership and accountability. Maybe you should try it sometime." Ethan's tone is playful, and his eyes shine brightly with enjoyment as he looks at me. "Can I get you a drink?"

The eye contact this man holds is mesmerizing.

"What are my options?"

"Let's go find out." Lightly gripping my elbow, he steers me to the private bar set up in the corner. The bartender smiles brightly as we approach.

"Hiya," she singsongs. "House drink is a cranberry

spritzer. We're also serving red and white wine, craft beers, and soda."

"What will it be, sweetheart?" Ethan asks with a smirk on his face.

"I'll try the cranberry spritzer, thank you."

"And I'll take a double IPA."

Lifting his hand, it hovers just above my shoulder, but he hesitates, like he's not sure if he should touch me. There's a silent question in his eye as he tentatively rubs his hand down my arm, burning a trail that leaves goose-bumps in its wake. When his hand reaches mine, he tangles our fingers together.

Leaning closer to my ear, he whispers, "Is this okay?"

There's a lump in my throat that I swallow before I speak. "That depends. Is it for show?"

He nods, his gaze penetrating through me.

"Then yes, it's okay."

No strings, no sex, I repeat my mantra in my head.

Why no sex? I groan inwardly.

Behind us, a loud squeal pulls us from the bubble we've inadvertently created for ourselves. Across the room, there's a man who looks like he's had one too many drinks, holding a microphone attached to a large speaker.

"Oh no," Ethan groans as the chords to "Sweet Caroline" begin, and the man twists the microphone around in his fingers for show.

"I want everybody to sing along with me!" the man yells into the mic. The melody floats through the speaker.

"I'm so sorry," Ethan shouts over the off-key singing.

The crowd starts to join in, and it's absolutely hilarious. My face hurts from smiling, and as the man hits the chorus, he turns the mic toward the crowd, and they join in screaming *bum bum bum*, and the energy is addictive.

Ethan sips his beer, and while he doesn't join in, I can tell by the way the corners of his mouth upturn that he's having a good time.

"No! You can't go. The night's still young!" Ethan's work best friend, Desmond, protests.

"You heard the man," Ethan says, dusting his fingertips across the top of my shoulder from where his arm is slung over the back of my chair. The party's still going strong, but it's almost eleven now, and we're going to get kicked out of here soon, anyway.

"I really can't stay," I insist, looking up at Ethan.

"Baby, it's cold outside!" Desmond sings, then slams his palms down on the table. "Another round of karaoke?"

"No, Des." Ethan laughs. "If my girl says she's got to go, she's got to go." Looking at me, he asks, "Have you ordered a ride already?"

"Not yet." Fishing my phone from my purse, I pull up the rideshare app and request a car. "Six minutes away."

"You're not going to drive her, Ethan?" a lithe woman named Ophelia asks, joining us from the next table over.

Our eyes meet briefly. "She's fiercely independent," he says, not knowing if it's true.

But it is. I have no choice but to be.

"He's right, plus I wouldn't want to steal him from you guys. The night's still young, as Desmond said."

"Another round, boys?" Ophelia asks the table.

All the men cheer except for Ethan.

"Here, let me walk you outside," he says, standing when I do.

I say my goodbyes to the people at our table, then lead the way to the doors.

When we've stepped just beyond the threshold of the restaurant, Ethan turns to me. "Thank you again, Holly. For everything."

My phone vibrates, and I glance down at the notification from the rideshare, alerting me that my ride is about to arrive.

"You didn't need me at all." I smile. "They love you."

He nods. "We're like a family. It's a blessing and a curse."

My heart tugs at the mention of family. With a tight smile, I say, "I imagine it could be."

Ethan steps closer to me, and I have to tilt my head back to look up at him. "You sure about the second stipulation in your bio?"

No strings. No sex.

It'd be so easy to go home with him, but that's a complication I don't need.

"I'm sure."

Brushing a fallen piece of hair from my face, he nods. "It was nice to meet you, Holly North."

"It was nice meeting you, Ethan Hanson."

Getting into the back of the car, the driver confirms my name, and I close the door while Ethan watches me.

There's a split second where I'm tempted to jump out of the car like I'm in a cheesy Christmas TV movie and leap into his arms to kiss him—let him take me home. But the thought is fleeting, and as the driver pulls back onto the street, I turn in my seat to glance at him one last time, and end up looking out the back window until Ethan is completely out of view.

Chapter Five

Message received

SUBJECT: HOLIDAY SOS

SO, WALMART OR TARGET?

-THE MOST ATTRACTIVE FAVORITE
STRANGER, AXEL

——

SUBJECT: HOLIDAY SOS

FOR WHAT?

-HOLLY

——

Message received

SUBJECT: HOLIDAY SOS

TO SHOP FOR OUR UGLY CHRISTMAS
SWEATERS. YOU ARE STILL ABLE TO COME
TOMORROW, RIGHT? I THOUGHT WE COULD
MEET UP IN THE MORNING AND I'LL BUY
YOU A LATTE AND THE MOST HIDEOUS
SWEATER IN YOUR STORE OF CHOICE.

-THE STRANGER YOU'LL NEVER BE CHILLY
WITH, AXEL

SUBJECT: HOLIDAY SOS

HMM. TARGET IS MY GO-TO, BUT I KNOW
WALMART HAS THE MORE OSTENTATIOUS
SWEATERS. LET'S GO TO WALMART. WHAT
TIME?

-HOLLY

Message received

SUBJECT: HOLIDAY SOS

HOW DOES AROUND 11 SOUND? SHOULD I
PICK YOU UP, OR DO YOU WANT TO MEET
THERE?

-YOUR STRANGER WHO'S NOT GOING TO
BE A STRANGER FOR LONG, AXEL

SUBJECT: HOLIDAY SOS

11 IS GREAT. LET'S MEET THERE. THERE'S A
COFFEE SHOP NEXT DOOR. SEE YOU
TOMORROW.

-HOLLY

"Wait, what do you mean I have to bake the pie
beforehand? I thought it was a pie baking

competition?" My eyes widen at Axel thanks to the bomb he just dropped on me.

He's easily the most carefree person I've ever met, and I've done nothing but laugh since we grabbed coffee and came to shop forty minutes ago.

"Well, it is, but this year my parents are hosting and didn't really think the whole baking part through. Their house could stand to be brought into the 2000s, but it's still hanging out in 1986. They have one oven, and I'm pretty sure it's older than me. Needless to say, baking is out of the question."

"How old are you?" I ask, pulling a tinsel filled sweater off the rack. There's a reindeer on it, and even some bells. I give it a little shake to see if they actually ring before putting it back where I found it.

"Twenty-eight."

Freezing with an ugly red and green monstrosity held midair, I give him a pointed look. "Your math ain't mathin'."

Axel grins widely at me and tugs a hanger from the rack. It's bright red with a green wreath and a stuffed Santa head coming out of the center of it. Honestly, it's mildly terrifying, but the smile on Axel's face makes up for it. "I think this might be the one."

"It's scary."

"It's *perfect*," he stresses, attempting to have a serious demeanor as he says it, but his eyes reflect otherwise.

Axel is handsome in an understated way, like his glow-up may not have happened until he reached his early twenties. When we met at the coffee shop, he walked in with purpose and I instantly knew it was him.

I must be pretty recognizable too, because he came right up and picked me up in a bear hug like he's known me for years.

I seem to have picked all the touchy feely men in San Diego. First Ethan, now Axel. Even Mateo kept finding ways to touch me. I wonder if Lincoln will be the same.

"Didn't you say you had nieces and nephews that would be there today? Are you trying to ruin Christmas for them?"

Picking up another option to wear, I'm pleased to see it's not bad. Red and green Christmas trees alternate lines on a cream-colored sweater, and a large-scale tree sits in the center.

It's actually kind of cute. I could wear my red sequin skirt with it, and champagne-colored ballet flats.

"No, no, no, no, no," Axel chants, shaking his head animatedly. "Do you want to *win*, or do you want to lose, Holly? Because that sweater tells me you want to lose, and I can tell by the twinkle in your eye this is your Christmas version of *Say Yes to the Dress*."

"How do you even know what *Say Yes to the Dress* is?" I laugh, flipping the sweater over my arm to carry.

It's mine. I'm taking it home.

He shrugs. "I have sisters. But seriously, we'll lose if you get that."

Taking the sweater from my arm, he holds it in the air and assesses it closer.

Reaching for it, I try to grab it back from his hold, but he spins to divert me from taking it.

I laugh. "Give me that back!" Reaching for the sweater, he pulls it just out of reach again, so I give up. "We won't lose, Axel. You haven't tasted my pie yet." My cheeks heat immediately, realizing that sounded like a sugarcoated innuendo.

His gaze sweeps over me before he waggles his eyebrows, not missing a beat. "Get your mind out of the gutter, North," he teases, nudging me softly in the ribs with his elbow. "C'mon, let's go pay for these and then split up for a while. We've got pies to bake and less than three hours before we need to meet up at my parents' house."

Sighing dramatically, even though I have a giant grin on my face, I relent and loop my arm through his while he guides us to the self-checkout lane.

"Hey, Ma!" Axel calls the moment we step over the threshold of the cozy, ranch-style home settled on the outskirts of La Mesa and Spring Valley. "I brought my famous pie! And my hot date."

Kicking off his shoes, he scoots them off to the side to accompany the several other pairs that have been left there, so I do the same as I look around the Harris' house.

Family pictures and home decor cover the walls, and from further in the home I hear laughter and children playing. The scents of cinnamon, cloves, and roasted meat fill the air as I follow Axel to the kitchen.

"Ma! I said I'm here with my famous pie and my hot date," Axel announces again as we join several adults gathered around a large kitchen table.

"Son! I didn't hear you come in," an older man with graying hair says, coming around to greet us. He's wearing a Christmas sweater with a smiley face emoji wearing a Santa hat on it, and is carrying a mug with a steaming beverage.

"Famous pie? Hot date? One of those things is false, and I can see it's not the date." A handsome man who looks similar to Axel, but with lighter hair, turns around from the table being used as you'd use a kitchen island, with his hand extended. "Hi, I'm Ridge, Axel's older, wiser, and more attractive brother."

"Holly," I greet, shifting my pie into my less dominant hand so I can shake his. "I'm pretty sure he's lying about the pie being famous. It looks too perfect, if you ask me."

"Hey!" Axel whines like he's a kid again. "Whose side are you on?"

"Here, give me that," Ridge says, grabbing the pie out of Axel's hands to inspect.

The energy between these two is palpable, as though every time they're together they revert back to a playful brotherhood.

A painful surge entangles my heart for a moment, but

the sadness doesn't linger. It can't—not with Axel's mom pushing back her sons to come speak to me.

"Hi, sweetheart. My name's Martha. I'm these two twits' momma." Martha opens her arms to me, and I hesitate before placing my pie on the counter and accepting her hug. "It's so nice to meet you."

"Nice to meet you, ma'am. Thank you for having me today."

"Oh, honey, thank you. Axel hasn't brought a woman home since the last one shattered his heart and ran off to Arizona with it."

"Ma," Axel growls, but she flicks her hand in his direction.

"You didn't make this pie," Ridge accuses, just as a few more people join us in the kitchen.

"What are we talking about?" a young woman asks, hopping onto a barstool. She looks similar to Axel and Ridge.

"Nothing," Axel says quickly, sending a glare at his brother at the same time Ridge says, "Axel's trying to cheat, *again*."

"No," the woman mocks, smacking her hand on her chest with gusto. "Not Axel!"

"Uncle Axel!" A little boy giggles as he sprints into the room, running so fast he nearly crashes into my legs. Instead, he uses them as a pole to swing around before shooting back out of the room.

"Hi, Jeremy!" Axel calls after him, but he's already gone.

"Jeremy, slow down! Hey, Ax," another woman says as she comes into the kitchen, going straight to him for a hug.

"Hey Care," he greets, smiling warmly. From over her shoulder, our eyes meet. "Carrie, this is Holly. Holly, my sister, Carrie."

"And Holly is?" She raises one eyebrow, her voice full of curiosity as she walks to me next. Without hesitation, she pulls me into a hug.

"My girl—date."

"Your girl date?" She laughs.

"Smooth, dipshit," Ridge chimes in.

"We haven't defined things yet," I insert, hugging Carrie, feeling the need to come to Axel's rescue even though I can tell it's all in good fun.

In my ear, she whispers, "If you need reinforcements, I've got you. These two can be relentless together. I'm not afraid to kick either of my brother's asses."

Immediately I like her, and as she rears back, she gives my shoulders a squeeze and winks. There's a smile on my lips when my gaze meets Axel's again. He's watching me with amusement as I meet his family one by one.

"So, I caught the tail end of that as I was coming in." Carrie looks over at Ridge. "What'd Axel do now?"

"Nothing," Axel grumbles. Picking up his pie, he starts to walk out of the kitchen. "C'mon, Holly. Let's go. I can see that they don't want us or our pies here."

"Oh, now, don't you wrap Holly into this, Axel! Ain't nothing wrong with her or her pie," Martha, Axel's mom, teases.

"Woooow," he groans. "I see how it is."

"Hey, that's not even a normal sized pie," the younger woman, who still hasn't been introduced, points out.

"Let me see it!" Carrie steps forward, grabbing the pie from Axel's hands. Trying to keep it in his grasp, he pulls it backward, but doesn't anticipate Carrie letting it go.

Within seconds, the pie lands upside down on the floor and is smashed within its plastic wrap.

"My pie!" Axel bends down to see if it's salvageable. Thankfully, it's been contained within its packaging, but it's turned into a giant mess.

"There's no way you baked that. They don't make household pie-pans that big." Ridge squats beside his brother to study the pie closer.

All the while, I watch from my place and lean against the table, trying not to laugh. My eyes track the movement of Axel's father as he walks over to a drawer by the refrigerator and pulls out a handful of forks. Passing them out, he then goes and picks up the smashed pie, placing it on the counter.

"Alright, everyone. Have a taste. If we're going to keep Axel's pie in the contest, we need to at least know if it's worth the kerfuffle."

"Ew, Dad, that was on the floor." Axel's younger sister wrinkles her nose in disgust, setting the fork down. "No way."

"Annie, it's still wrapped in plastic. It's fine."

"C'mon, Holly, we still have time to make a run for it," Axel jests, coming up behind me.

"No way! I'm invested now. I need to know if you cheated." I giggle, swatting at Axel's chest playfully. It's sort of an intimate gesture, but Axel feels like an old friend.

Holding my fork expectantly, Axel's dad peels back the plastic and in unison, we both, along with Carrie, and Ridge, dig into the smooth, deep orange pie.

The room is silent as we take our bites. Delicious, sweet pumpkin explodes on my taste buds, with notes of cloves, cinnamon, and nutmeg.

"Definitely store bought," Ridge concludes.

Nodding her head, Carrie agrees. "Yeah, you didn't make this."

"It's Costco," I hum, and shamelessly dig my fork in for another bite. "I'd recognize a Costco pumpkin pie anywhere."

"Wow, cool, thanks everyone for ganging up on the best baker ever to grace this family." Axel tosses his hands into the air, his voice full of sarcasm. Turning to Martha, he swings his arm over her shoulder, and tosses me a quick wink. "What's my prize, Ma? You all know I won. Nothing beats Costco pie."

A bubble of laughter rises through me as I watch the exchange.

This is how my family was. I've *missed* this.

So many pieces of me were terrified to go on these holiday dates with these men—being around their loving families, their co-workers—I was afraid it would hurt so badly and cause the hole in my chest to widen further.

But being here, in a family that clearly loves each other

so much, and is willing to accept strangers into their home with open arms, gives me a slight shift in my perspective.

My heart aches, but the Harris family has also healed something in me, just like Mateo and his date did, and that's a Christmas gift in and of itself.

Chapter Six

"Mrow," Potato vocalizes as he slaps his paw against my face. My eyes crack open, and I recognize the heaviness from where he sits on my chest. "Mrow."

"Ugh, Potato. Too early." Turning onto my side, I pull my comforter up to my chin as I push the feline form of a chicken nugget off me in one quick motion. Rather than flee, he simply slides off with a *plop* onto the mattress. Feeling his beady little eyes watching me, I growl obnoxiously at my cat. "Why must you be so demanding?"

Pushing my blankets off, I get out of bed and walk into the kitchen with my eyes barely open. A giant yawn pulls from my body as I open a can of wet food for him and spoon it into his bowl. The automatic feeder next to it is still full, but apparently the sky will fall if Potato doesn't get his wet food by the crack of dawn.

Glancing at the clock, I see that it's actually past nine

in the morning, but regardless. It's Christmas Eve. I'm allowed to sleep in on Christmas Eve.

For a moment I contemplate getting back in bed, and think about my comforter, so cozy and inviting. My bedding is probably still warm.

Instead of opting to fall back into my warm cocoon of blankets, I make a stop by the thermostat to crank up the heater, before heading to the coffeemaker. Flipping it on, I know I really should get a jumpstart on my day. I'm set to meet Lincoln at a nearby coffee shop in an effort to get to know him a little before traveling an hour away to spend the evening with his family. I'm a little nervous about the road conditions—it's been raining in San Diego for the last three days straight, and I know Julian has gotten a lot of snow.

I'm also nervous about meeting Lincoln. It may be a little presumptuous to assume that I'm going to like him, based on his profession and the way he has written to me in his messages, but something about him gives me a good feeling, and I'm curious to see what he's like in person.

Turning on another Christmas movie, I sit on the couch and let my mind go numb as I watch the beautiful redhead heroine in the movie wander through the snow. It's insane how much *my* life feels like a Christmas movie right now, with all of these crazy dates I have been on.

When the coffee maker indicates that it is ready, I pour a cup in my favorite holiday mug, and give myself time to sip it before I need to go get ready.

Potato watches me from the bathroom door, judging

me silently as I put on bright red lipstick, and pull my blonde hair up into a ponytail.

"Mrow," he complains again, and I turn to look at him with my foundation brush in hand, pointing it in his direction.

"You stop that," I scold, even though it's really not scolding at all when speaking to a cat. "I just filled your bowl. Go eat your dry food."

He doesn't, though. Instead, he continues to sit in the doorway and watch as I finish getting ready. By the time I put on my jeans and holiday sweater—this one much cuter than the one I wore last weekend with Axel—Potato has curled up in a ball on the bathroom rug and is fast asleep.

Must be nice, I think to myself.

With one final check in the mirror, I grab my purse and I'm out the door, hopping into my car as quickly as I can so I don't get drenched by the rain. Letting the car warm up, I flip through the radio stations to find the one playing popular Christmas music, and turn it up, trying to get myself in the holiday spirit.

This week has been hard mentally. The closer it's crept to Christmas, the heavier my heart has felt. With no family to buy gifts for this year, I decided to pick up a few small trinkets to bring to Lincoln's, not only so I don't show up empty-handed, but so I'd have a sense of normalcy.

Pulling into the coffee shop parking lot, I'm not surprised to find that it's nearly empty, and when I enter the building, there's only one other person there, an older gentleman, working on his laptop.

With Lincoln nowhere in sight, I go ahead and order my drink.

The barista greets me with a lovely smile. "Merry Christmas Eve! What can I get for you?"

"I'll have a caramel brûlée latte, please."

"What size?"

"16 ounces is fine, thank you."

As she rings me up, I turn around to see if anyone has pulled into the parking lot, but there's still no sign of Lincoln.

Heading to a table in the corner, I take the seat that faces the window so I can keep an eye out for him. A few minutes later, the barista brings me my coffee, setting it, and a lid, down on the table in front of me.

Wrapping my hands around the steaming to-go cup, I smile down at it. The barista created a beautiful Christmas tree in the foam, and I almost feel guilty drinking it.

As I sip my coffee, the minutes tick by, and with each one that passes I start to feel a sense of dread, wondering if I'm being stood up. I've only been here for 15 minutes, but I haven't heard from Lincoln since we decided on a time and place for this initial meeting.

When my coffee is nearly finished, I decide to go order another, even though I also had a cup at home.

It's Christmas after all, and I have a long day ahead.

Once I'm standing, I see an all black Range Rover fly

into the parking lot, coming to a stop in a spot right in front. A man gets out and rushes inside.

The moment the doors open, our eyes meet, and I know instantly that it's Lincoln. Still wearing his navy blue scrubs, his hair is disheveled, and he looks absolutely exhausted. Despite that, he's extremely handsome, with dirty blond hair and green eyes.

He doesn't hesitate to approach me, already talking before he's even crossed the room.

"Holly! I am so sorry I'm late. I ended up pulling a double and performing an emergency surgery that took all night. I just left the hospital."

"Why didn't you just cancel on me?" I ask, completely surprised that he's standing in front of me right now after working, if I had to guess, close to twenty hours.

"I wouldn't cancel on you." He flashes me a lopsided grin, and extends his hand. "Hi. I'm Lincoln, by the way."

Shaking it, I can't help but notice how warm his palm is in contrast with mine. I'm always freezing. "I figured as much. But you must be exhausted…"

"I am, but this is important."

I blush at his words and the heavy eye contact he's giving me right now, like he's peering directly into my soul. It makes me a little uncomfortable, but at the same time, my curiosity is piqued.

"Have you been here long?" he asks.

"Not long. I got here early," I lie. "I'm not a fan of driving in the rain, so I gave myself a little too much time to get here."

"That was smart. The roads are a mess. What can I get you to drink?"

"Another caramel brûlée latte would be great, just a small one, though. I've already had enough for the day."

"Coming right up." As Lincoln heads to the counter to order our drinks, I go back to the table and sit, finishing the one I had from earlier while I wait for him to join me.

When he walks over with both of our beverages a couple minutes later, I take mine gratefully, and smile when I see another Christmas tree in the foam.

"The designs are cute," he comments, holding his cup out for me to look at. "Mine's a snowman."

"I didn't know they did designs like this! I feel a little guilty. Usually, when I come here, I take it to go, and the lid is already on."

"I don't think they do this all the time. I've been here a few times too, and I've never noticed anything like this."

"Hmm, maybe it's because it's Christmas Eve."

He takes a sip of his coffee, then connects his gaze with mine. "Thank you for coming. I feel bad taking you away from your family on Christmas Eve, but mine is relentless in their pursuit of finding me a wife."

"Not interested?"

"Not at this time. I'm focused on my career, and even though I would love to have a family someday, that day hasn't come yet. No matter how much I explain that to my parents, they still keep asking me for a daughter-in-law and grandchildren." He takes another sip of his drink.

"That must be frustrating," I say, validating his feelings. I don't touch on the topic of him taking me away from my family on Christmas Eve. No sense in ruining the mood when I just met him.

"So what do you do, Holly North? Tell me everything I need to know about my stand-in girlfriend. Or what did you say in your bio? Holidate?"

We share a smile at my play on words.

"Well, there's not much to tell. I am the manager at a bookstore. My best friend, and roommate, is an overweight cat named Potato. He's brown, so the name is quite fitting."

"That's it?"

"For now."

"That's fair."

We both wear coy smiles as we stop to take sips of our drinks, and I shyly avert his gaze, looking around the quiet coffee shop instead.

"So, you're sure you're comfortable with today? I know Julian isn't exactly close, and the roads are a bit messy," Lincoln asks considerately before taking another gulp.

"I'll be fine. I don't *love* it, but I'll just take my time while on the road."

"I'm so sorry I can't drive you. I wish I hadn't promised my parents I'd stay over, but it also means I would have had to drive into the mountains two days in a row."

"Yeah, that doesn't make any sense!" I exclaim a little too enthusiastically. I set my cup on the table, but to my dismay, I accidently place the edge of it on a piece of the wood that's slightly higher than the rest, and before I know what's happening, my latte spills everywhere.

I gasp, pushing to my feet as the liquid rolls from the table into my lap. "Oh, my gosh!"

Lincoln springs into action, tossing napkins all around the table to absorb the mess.

"Are you okay? Did it burn you?"

Shaking my head, I start to dab at the coffee on my pants. "No, it cooled off, thank God."

"Good. Here, let me go grab more napkins."

As Lincoln walks to the counter, I look down at my soaked jeans and inwardly groan.

Of course, this happened.

"I'm so sorry," I tell him, taking the napkins from his hand when he returns. "I'm so embarrassed."

"Don't be! It happens to the best of us. Honestly, I'm surprised it wasn't me who did it." He tries to stifle a yawn at the end of his sentence, but is unsuccessful. "I'm sorry, that was incredibly rude."

"Don't be sorry, you're exhausted. Look, I'm covered in coffee, you're about three seconds away from falling asleep at this table. Why don't we go our separate ways and I'll see you up at your parents' house in a few hours? Three o'clock, right?"

"Yes. Thank you, Holly. I'm so sorry I'm lousy company right now. I wasn't planning on working a double last night."

"Saving lives is more important than a coffee date, Lincoln. Trust me, I'm not offended in the least."

"So, I'll see you later, then?" he asks, and it's as though he's feeling a little...shy? Maybe out of his element is the better phrase.

I can tell he's the type of man who usually oozes confidence, but right now, it's almost like the boyish side has come out and he's unsure of this whole situation.

Same, buddy, same.

Nodding my head, I smile. "Of course."

I grab my purse at the same time he says, "Let me walk you out."

With his hand on the middle of my back, Lincoln guides me out of the coffee shop and to my car. The rain has picked up again, so our exchange is short, with more promises of seeing each other later.

I stay in the parking lot until he drives away, then I turn my car on and head back to my apartment to hang out with Potato until it's time for me to leave again.

Chapter Seven

Message received

SUBJECT: HOW MANY MESSAGES HAVE
YOU RECEIVED?

THANKS AGAIN FOR WAITING FOR ME THIS
MORNING, DESPITE ME BEING LATE.
LOOKING FORWARD TO SEEING YOU THIS
AFTERNOON. DRIVE CAREFULLY.

LINCOLN STOKES

My house is nearly silent as I sit on my couch petting Potato, rereading the message Lincoln sent me a few minutes ago. A strange feeling settles in the pit of my stomach—not quite nerves, but not butterflies either.

Lincoln is sweet, and I'm curious to see what being around his family will be like. I'd be lying if I said the idea of pretending I'm dating a doctor isn't fun, especially one as handsome as he is.

Going into the kitchen, I refill Potato's automatic feeder and water and spoon out a can of wet food into his bowl in case I'm home later than anticipated. I've been watching the weather app, and it's been snowing consistently in Julian today.

Walking to my bedroom, I flip on the light in my closet and pull out a pair of dark wash denim jeans, my cream-colored puffer jacket and matching beanie, and my black boots. I'm wearing a thin, hunter green sweater, and Lincoln specifically told me not to dress up, so I'm content with my choice of outfit. It'll be comfortable to drive in and appropriate enough for a casual dinner.

When it's time to go, I grab my things, then take a few moments while inside the car to set up my GPS with the Stokes' address. Gripping the wheel tightly, I give myself a pep talk as I hit the road.

You can do this. This is the last date. It's going to be fine. I'm just going to enjoy a nice dinner with a family, pretend to be a doctor's girlfriend, and I'll be back home with Potato before I know it.

Traffic is light as I head out of town and toward the mountains. The scenery passes by, changing from straight city roads to winding country ones. The further in elevation I climb, the more I start to see the evidence of the winter storm, starting with dirty, black slush, then transforming into vibrant white snow.

Finally, when I enter the town of Julian, my mouth falls. The small town has transformed into something out of a Hallmark Christmas movie. Light poles are adorned with garland and bows. Every business has their windows painted with holiday spirit, and I can tell as soon as the sun goes down that this main strip will be covered in multicolored lights.

The roads are freshly plowed, with crisp banks of snow hugging the curbs. The town is small, and as I get closer to the Stokes' home, I start to get nervous.

What if they don't like me?

Not that it really matters, since I'll never see them again after today, but still. The thought bothers me, but the potential of letting Lincoln down bothers me more.

Making a left on the street the GPS is directing me to turn on, I smile as I pass by a tree farm, and strain to get a look at it while driving by. Less than a quarter of a mile later, I turn into a small gravel driveway and park alongside the black Range Rover I recognize from earlier.

Killing the engine, I reach into the passenger seat and grab my jacket, putting it on while still sitting in the warmth of my car. By the time I get out, a light snow has started again, and Lincoln comes out of the house with a wide grin on his face. Slamming my car door, I start toward him.

"Holly! You made it! How was the drive?"

"Not bad!" Pulling my jacket tight around me, I look at the quaint home and yard behind him. "It's beautiful here. Did you grow up in this house?"

"No, we lived in the city when I was a kid, but once I was out on my own and in medical school, my parents decided they wanted a slower lifestyle."

"Julian is perfect for that." It's hard to believe I haven't been up here since I was a kid. My parents took me and my brother to the pumpkin patch once, but I can't recall any other adventures up this way.

"Wait until you try the famous pie, too. My mom picked up a couple for tonight." He extends his arm for me to take, so I do, letting him steer me to the house.

"Sounds delicious, I love pie."

The screen door creaks as he opens it and turns the knob to the main door, pushing it open. "Mom, Dad, Holly is here," he calls as we enter, leading me into the living room where his parents are playing a card game together.

His dad sits in a recliner while his mom has her legs crossed, sitting on the floor. Both hold a hand of cards, but when his mom sees me, her face lights up.

"Is this her?" She tosses her cards to the side, getting up from the floor as quickly as possible. "Oh, Linc, she's a looker!"

With her hand extended, she practically runs in my direction. "Hi! I'm Tina, Lincoln's mom."

"Hi, Tina. So nice to meet you. Thank you so much for having me in your beautiful home." Turning to his father, I close the distance between us and offer my hand. "Hi, I'm Holly."

He takes my hand in his as he uses the arm of the recliner to push himself to a stand. "Tim," he says. "Nice to meet you, darlin'."

"We are so thrilled that you could spend Christmas Eve

with us, Holly! Linc is our only son, and I'm not embarrassed to say that I have been hounding him to settle down. It's so good to see he's finally putting himself out there."

"And I've been explaining to you for years, Mother, that I will get back in the dating pool, once I'm ready to shift some of my focus from my job."

"Seems like the dating pool is ready to have you back, son." His father chuckles.

"Come, come. Sit, sit." Tina gestures to the couch. "Let's cut right to the cute stuff—tell me how you two met! Linc hasn't told me anything, and I am dying to hear all about it."

Panicked, I look over at Lincoln, begging him with my eyes to help. Thankfully, he takes the reins, because I'm certainly not prepared to bald-face lie to his parents within three minutes of entering their home.

"Holly manages a bookstore. I went in on my break one afternoon, and the rest was history."

"Give an old lady a break!" his mom chastises. "Certainly there's more to it than that."

"Not really, Mom. I got into the checkout line, our eyes met, and I couldn't leave without a date."

A smile plays on his lips, and I mirror it. "It's not hard to imagine why I said yes. You have raised a very kind man, Mr. and Mrs. Stokes."

"Oh, please. Mr. and Mrs. Stokes were my father and mother, please call us Tina and Tim," Lincoln's father requests.

"Have you two been dating long?" Tina asks, with a million questions reflected in her chestnut brown eyes.

Lincoln meets my gaze again, but this time I play into the story. "Not too long—what's it been? A month?"

"Hmm," he hums. "A little less, but knowing Holly is like knowing an old friend. It's like we've known each other forever."

Tina scrunches her nose when he calls me a friend, but doesn't say anything. Instead, she asks, "Are you two hungry? Thirsty? Dinner will be at five."

"I'd love a drink."

"Perfect! We have sodas and sparkling waters in the garage fridge. Or I can get you a glass of wine, eggnog, or cider."

"Eggnog sounds delicious," I respond excitedly. I love eggnog, but I couldn't bring myself to buy any this year, knowing Miles wouldn't be around to help me drink it.

"Linc?" Tina questions.

"I'll have the same, Mom, thank you. Can I help?"

"No, no! Take over my game with your father, and I'll be right back."

Leaning into me, Linc presses his lips against the side of my hair so it looks like he's giving me a kiss, and whispers, "This is going great, thank you."

"You're welcome," I whisper back, smiling up at him.

The Stokes family is so welcoming, just like I had a feeling they would be, and I feel grateful to be spending my Christmas Eve with them. If I can't spend it with my own family, at least being in the presence of another family makes the holiday not feel so empty.

With a small gasp, I turn to Lincoln. "I bought gifts for your family, and left them in the car! I'll be right back, I'm going to get them."

"Do you want me to come with you?"

"No! I'll be fine."

When I step outside, I am surprised to see the light snowfall has turned into thick flurries, the snow raining down hard and fast. Wrapping my jacket tighter around my torso, I run to the car to grab the presents, nearly tripping over my boots, then hurry back inside.

Snowflakes cling to my jacket and hair, and my teeth chatter from the cold.

"It's getting pretty ugly out there!" I say to Tina as she emerges from the kitchen.

"The snow has been very unpredictable these last couple days! But I was just looking at the weather app, and it's supposed to stop shortly, and be clear for the rest of the evening."

"Good to know." I shrug off my jacket, and hang it on the coatrack.

"Interested in a round of rummy?" Tina asks with a quirk of her brow, handing me my eggnog.

"Absolutely!"

Looping her arm through mine, she leads me back to the living room and says, "I think we're gonna get along just fine, dear."

Zee

Chapter Eight

I can't remember the last time I laughed so much. Lincoln's family is amazing, and I've had the best afternoon getting to know them. Between helping his mom in the kitchen, and her insisting that we sit in front of the fire and watch a Christmas movie while stringing popcorn garland, it almost feels like home.

"Are you ready?" Lincoln asks with a coy smile. Winding his arm back, he lets a piece of popcorn launch, and I try to catch it in my mouth, failing miserably as it tumbles down my shirt instead.

Laughing, I pick up one of my own. "That was a terrible shot, let me show you how it's done."

The popcorn goes flying as a warm feeling embeds in my heart.

Picking up another cranberry, I string it onto my garland strand, continuing the pattern that I've been working on.

"You seem like an old garland pro," Tim comments, watching me as he strings his popcorn on his own strand.

With a smile, I tell him, "This isn't my first rodeo."

"Old family tradition?"

"Something like that." Wanting to change the subject, I ask, "What about you guys? What other family traditions do you have for Christmas?"

"When Lincoln was little," his mom interjects, "we used to make hot cocoa and drive around to look at lights every Christmas Eve. Now that he is grown, our Christmas Eves look a lot like this, which is just fine by me."

"It's been a great day, thank you so much again for having me."

"Oh darling, the pleasure is ours! When Lincoln told us he was bringing someone home to meet us, we were thrilled. Even though he warned us that it is very new, we are so grateful just to meet you."

A wave of guilt washes into me, and I look over at Lincoln for reassurance. He offers me a tight smile, the guilt clearly wearing on him, too.

Changing the subject, he says, "Mom, dinner smells delicious. How much longer do you think we have?"

"Oh! I think it's probably all set to go now. Why don't we get it set up?"

"Let me help!" Pushing to my feet, I abandon my popcorn garland and follow Tina into the kitchen.

Handing me a pair of oven mitts and a stack of potholders, she tasks me to lay them out on the kitchen table, then grab the casserole dishes. Christmas Eve dinner is all the traditional holiday foods and everything smells divine.

One by one, we arrange candied yams, mashed potatoes, stuffing, macaroni and cheese, green bean casserole, corn, turkey, and cranberry sauce onto the rustic dining room table. It's a feast for an army, not a family of three and a guest.

"I hope your pants are stretchy." Tim chuckles, walking into the dining room. He pats his stomach for good measure.

"Wow, Mom, this is way too much food, as usual. Anything I can grab to help?" Lincoln asks, following his dad.

"Nope," Tina singsongs. "Holly and I got everything! Please, everyone, sit. Let's eat while it's hot."

We fall into easy conversation, and Lincoln tells us stories from the hospital. The table is howling with laughter as Tim pivots into a tale of him and his buddy shoveling snow out of some neighbor's driveway when his friend slipped and seemingly fell in slow motion like a cartoon character. It was all fun and games until Tim revealed they had to call an ambulance for a broken tailbone, and then Lincoln went into full doctor mode, peppering his dad with questions.

As Lincoln speaks, I find myself daydreaming about a potential life with him. It's easy to envision myself in this family, but I can't see Lincoln as anything other than a friend. He's attractive, but not in the 'I want to rip his clothes off' type of way. More in the 'I'm proud to call him my hot best friend' kind of way.

Shaking away the thought, I turn my attention to the picturesque scene through the window adjacent to where I sit and watch snowflakes fall. It truly is a winter wonderland just beyond the glass. A white Christmas.

"Looks like the snow is picking up again." Tina touches my arm, pulling my focus back to the table. "I'd feel much better if you slept here tonight, if you're comfortable with it. You shouldn't be out on the roads after dark in weather like this."

"Oh! I really can't stay..." my voice trails off as I look out the window again. "I'll be okay, but thank you so much."

"If you change your mind, the offer stands." She pats my arm again before picking up her fork.

"I appreciate it."

We finish our meals, and it's the most full I've felt, in both my stomach and my heart, in months.

"Let's wait a while for dessert, dear. I can't breathe at the moment," Tim tells Tina as she begins clearing dishes from the table. He lets out a long breath, as though that will help make some room.

"Yes, I was thinking maybe in thirty minutes or so." She squeezes his shoulder.

"Excellent."

"I'm so sorry, I have to take this—it's the hospital," Lincoln tells us, looking down at his vibrating phone. He pushes to his feet and hurries out of the room.

"Can I help?" I offer Tina, who's now on her second trip to the kitchen.

"No thanks, sweetheart, you go relax. I enjoy doing dishes. It's my 'me' time."

Tim's already moved to his recliner and is settling in. Looking out the window again, I get the crazy urge to go enjoy the snow. I hardly ever see it—it's not like it snows in San Diego.

"I'm going to go for a short walk," I tell Lincoln's mom as I grab my puffer jacket from the coatrack. Taking my beanie from the pocket, I tug it onto my head, then shrug on my jacket.

"Be careful out there, sweetheart, the snow can pick up fast," she mothers, and it simultaneously warms my heart and shatters it.

"Will do, don't worry about me. I won't be gone long. Just want to walk off dinner a little."

"Sounds like a plan. Make some room for dessert."

"Be back soon."

Zipping my jacket, I pull open the front door and step outside. The cold air kisses my cheeks and the tip of my nose, as frosty flurries rain down around me. Pulling my beanie down a little further, I cross my arms and start walking, deciding to go in the direction of the tree farm I passed on my way here.

Zee

Chapter Nine

The soft flakes fall lightly around me as my boots leave indentations in the snow cover with every step. It takes about two minutes of being outside of the Stokes home before grief settles into the depths of my bones and pulls me under.

Tears stream down my face as I walk, and I will them to go away, silently begging for them to give me a break just this *one* time.

I don't want to be sad.

I want to bask in the merriment of the holiday and enjoy my time with the wonderful family who invited me into their home.

But grief is a double-edged sword, cutting deep with the smallest of thoughts.

Blowing out a shaky breath, I wipe at the tears and pull myself together in the last few steps it takes me to reach the Christmas tree farm.

Forcing myself to focus on the perfect Christmas postcard scenery instead of the anguish brewing inside, I stop just before the entrance and take it all in.

White string lights line the fence posts, while large light towers illuminate the farm like a beacon, letting the population of Julian know they're still open for business, despite it being almost seven p.m. on Christmas Eve.

Most of the precut Christmas trees are protected under a giant event tent, but there is a large selection of snow-covered trees still in-ground and ready to be cut.

Crossing under the Ryan Family Tree Farm sign, I make a beeline to the tent, wanting to get out of the below-freezing temperatures.

When I step inside, I'm immediately engulfed in the delicious scent of pine, and hints of coffee and cinnamon from the nearby snack bar. It's quiet—only a few other people are looking around. There's a family selecting a last-minute tree to embellish their home, and a young woman sitting on top of a picnic table, looking at something just out of view.

The tent is much warmer than the frigid air outside, so I unzip my jacket just slightly, and wiggle my hands free from my gloves, shoving them into my pocket. Walking around, I look at the different trees, letting my fingers brush against the needles.

My phone vibrates in my pocket and pulls my attention, so I take it out and see a new message from Lincoln.

Message received

Subject: How many messages have you received?

Are you okay? I came back from my call and my parents said you went for a walk. I hope we didn't scare you off...

Let me know if you want company. See you soon?

-Lincoln

Quickly, I respond, letting him know that I'm fine and will be back shortly, but he doesn't need to come find me. Truly, I don't intend on being here long. I should probably think about getting back on the road, anyway. I hate driving at night, and in these conditions, I know it will take me even longer to get back down the mountain.

While I walk, I catch up on the messages I missed from friends wishing me a Merry Christmas. As I type out a response to my friend and coworker, Genesis, I lose all sense of awareness, and before I understand what's happening, I feel my entire body lurch forward. Attempting to catch myself, I spin wildly, grabbing onto the branch of a nearby tree.

But it's too late to keep from falling, and I end up crashing onto the cold hard dirt, landing flat on my back.

As if that isn't enough, at the same time as I end up on the ground, the worst noise in the world begins to clatter around me.

Disoriented, I lift my head to see what's happening and am instantly mortified as I watch the domino effect of fir trees falling one by one.

"Are you okay?" a man shouts and rushes over, coming around from behind another row of trees.

His eyes widen as he takes in what is happening, and springs into action, wrapping his arm around the tree closest to him so it doesn't fall.

Single-handedly, he's able to stop them, and when he is sure the trees are stable, he rushes to my side.

I feel like I'm seeing double, but it's not a bad sight to behold. The man is ruggedly handsome, with messy hair that's overgrown, and facial scruff that adds to his features. His deep brown eyes have a beautiful glow beneath the lighting in the tent, and make me feel like they're staring into my soul. He wears a red plaid shirt, and jeans that are slightly dirty from the long day's work. He's the epitome of a man who lives in the mountains, and my cheeks flush as every spicy lumberjack book I've ever read comes crashing into my mind.

I'm hot and bothered as I sit here ogling the man, suddenly all too aware I'm laying in the dirt after falling exceptionally ungracefully, with this plaid-wearing Adonis staring down at me.

"What happened?" I ask, a little confused. Trying to sit up, the man touches my shoulder and gently pushes me back down.

"Hang on, not too fast there, Snow Angel. You might have a concussion." The deep baritone rumble of his voice sends a shiver down my spine that somehow lands in my stomach and sends a wave of warm arousal down to my core.

"I do not have a concussion!" I argue, wanting to put

some distance between me and this man before I pull him down on top of me.

Maybe I do have a concussion—what are these thoughts?

Pushing upward again to try to sit, I notice a bright yellow extension cord lying over my boot.

Oh God, I must've tripped.

Looking over at the Christmas tree wreckage, I blow out a frustrated breath. There are at least four trees that have fallen and are lying on the dirt floor, just like me.

The man follows my line of sight and starts to laugh. "You really did a number on my trees there."

"Your trees?"

"Last time I checked."

"You own this place or something?" I close my eyes, rubbing my temples.

This is so embarrassing.

"Do you have a headache?" he asks, his voice laced with concern.

"A small one, but I don't think it's from the fall."

"Do you want to try to stand?"

"Yes, please."

The man pushes to his feet and holds his hand out for me to grab. Slowly, he helps me up, but the second I put pressure on my ankle, I feel a throb.

Hissing, I grit my teeth. "I think I may have twisted my ankle."

"Let's go take a look." Guiding my arm over his shoulder, he wraps his arm around my waist and helps me hobble over to a nearby picnic table.

"What's your name?" he asks as we move slowly across the tented area.

"Zee."

"Zee? That's not a name. That's a letter," he teases.

"It's short for Elizabeth." I hiss again as my good foot steps on a rock and slides slightly against the dirt. "What's yours?"

"Miller. Miller Ryan."

"So the man making fun of my name has a last name for a first name. Sounds about right."

He grins, and my heart does a weird flip-flop.

"Easy does it," he coaxes, guiding me down to the bench. When I'm seated, he turns my body to prop my leg up, then proceeds to unzip my boot.

Reaching for my wool sock, he pulls it down. "Is this okay?"

"Yeah." I nod. "Go ahead."

"Is she alright?" the woman at the other table calls out to Miller.

He feels around at various parts of my ankle, looking at it carefully as he alternates pressures, gauging my reaction. "Yeah, Tamar. I think she'll survive it."

"Doesn't need emergency surgery? A tourniquet?" I tease, my thoughts drifting back to Lincoln. Maybe I should ask him to look at it.

Pulling my sock back in place, Miller lets the elastic gently snap against my skin. "An ice pack should suffice. I'll be right back."

"Okay, thank you." I smile up at him as he stands, and

watch him walk away, wondering why there's a heaviness in me with every step he takes.

He peeks over his shoulder a couple of times, grinning whenever our eyes meet, until finally, he turns past a line of trees, in the direction of the snack bar, and then out of my sight.

Miller

Chapter Ten

There's a strange sensation in my stomach whirling around as I walk away from the woman who just managed to topple over almost an entire line of Christmas trees.

Interestingly enough, I secured the extension cord with a rubber mat, specifically so no one would trip over it, but she somehow found a small part of it that wasn't covered.

Bad luck? Or is this typical for the woman with a letter for a name?

Christmas Eve is arguably the slowest day of the season, so having her wander in, especially on such a snowy evening, is bewildering. I'd be lying if I said she didn't capture my attention from the moment I saw her, though.

First of all, she's stunning.

Second of all—what an entrance.

I want to know more about her, but I shrug the thought away as quickly as it came.

Going behind the snack bar, I turn to Reed, the high school kid I hired for seasonal work. "Hey, could you make me a hot chocolate real quick, please?"

Heading over to the ice chest, I dig in the cold to see if I can find a random ice pack. Coming up short, I end up grabbing a plastic bag and shovel a handful of cubes into it instead—it'll have to suffice.

Waiting a couple of minutes for Reed to finish making the hot chocolate, I watch as he combines the chocolate mix with the milk he just steamed, stirring the steaming beverage together. When he's finished, he puts the lid on and hands it to me with a curt nod.

"Thanks. Why don't you go ahead and get out of here? There's only one family left, anyway, and then I'm closing up."

"Are you sure, boss?" he asks hesitantly, glancing at his watch to confirm the time.

"Absolutely, kid. Have a good holiday. And get home safe."

"Will do! Have a good Christmas."

We both walk out of the snack bar area at the same time, heading in opposite directions. Coming around a row of Christmas trees, the strange sensation in my stomach flutters around again the second Zee is back in view.

Damn butterflies.

I've never had an immediate reaction to a woman before and it's slightly unnerving. But if I could have drawn a picture of my ideal lady, I never would have imagined she'd come to life and be sitting at my picnic table right this minute.

The closer I get, the more nervous I become.

Wanting to make a good impression, I hurry over to her, holding the ice in the air as I do. "Couldn't find an ice pack, but this is practically the same."

She smiles, and it radiates through my entire body.

What the hell is going on?

"Thank you." Her voice is soft and feminine, and her eyes light up as she watches me press the ice to her sock, not wanting to put it directly on her skin.

Our gaze meets, and it feels like time stands still as I get lost in her eyes.

From my peripheral, I see someone shift, and remember that we're not alone. Looking over at Tamar, I nod toward the exit. "We're all good here if you want to go home, Tamar. I'll close up in a few minutes. Already sent Reed home."

"I don't mind waiting so you don't close alone," she says, and while I appreciate the gesture, I'm hoping to have the opportunity to get to know Elizabeth during whatever time we have together, without an audience.

"It's all good. Really. Get home safe and have a good holiday." I grin at her, then look down at Zee's ankle, shifting the ice.

With no room to argue further, Tamar stands and

comes over to give me a hug before she heads out. "Merry Christmas."

After I return the sentiment, she turns to leave.

"Girlfriend?" the cute blonde next to me whispers, her eyes shimmering with mischief as we watch Tamar exit the tent.

"Nah, just an old friend."

"You sure about that?" She laughs. "Because friends don't glare at random women in pain, being helped by a stranger, unless they have some sort of attachment to said stranger."

"What did she do?"

"Nothing," she shrugs, "she just glared at me while I sat here. I tried to engage in some small talk, but she didn't seem interested, and I know when to take a hint. She doesn't seem like the type of woman you want to piss off."

"Ha! Been there."

"What'd *you* do?"

"At the risk of sounding like a sleazeball, we *were* involved at one point, but she broke it off when she realized I wasn't interested in a relationship."

"A woman who stands by what she wants. I like it." She sounds like she's proud of Tamar.

"Well, if it makes you feel better, she tossed me out on my ass and in only my boxers, too."

Elizabeth roars a laugh, tossing her head back as though she can envision just that. "Damn, you must've pissed her off."

"Yeah, I learned real quick not to mess with her, and

definitely not tell her I didn't want anything serious while still in her bed."

"Ah, what valuable lessons to learn. You shouldn't do that to *any* woman. Good for her!"

"Yeah, not so good for me, though."

"But it serves you right," she muses.

"Mmm hmm." I feign a stern look. "What are you doing out this far in the mountains on Christmas Eve, anyway?"

"How do you know I don't live here?" she counters.

"Trust me, I'd know it if you did."

Our eyes meet again, and it practically takes my breath away.

Why does she have to be so gorgeous?

Especially since she doesn't live here.

"Why are you looking at me like that?" she asks quietly.

"Like what?" I grumble, averting my gaze. Focusing on her ankle, I shift the ice.

But she doesn't press further. Instead, she changes the subject. "So what's the verdict? You think I can walk on the sucker?"

"More than likely. It doesn't seem to be broken, obviously, and honestly, it doesn't seem to be sprained either. You probably just landed on it wrong and twisted it a little. Do you want to try standing?"

"Sure." She accepts my hand and I help lift her to her feet.

"How does it feel?"

"Not great, but not terrible, either. I should be fine. Thank you so much for your help. I'm so sorry I knocked over the trees. Can I help you put them back upright?"

I shrug. "I'm not gonna deal with it until after the holiday. We're not open tomorrow, so it doesn't need to look pretty."

"What do you do with all the trees that aren't sold?" She lifts her foot into the air so she can gently move it around, testing how it feels.

"Take them back home and chop them up. Prep them for firewood. Donate them, if anyone wants a tree after Christmas. That kind of thing."

"That's cool." She pushes her hands in her pockets, looking down, as though she isn't sure what to do next.

Part of me wants to invite her to stay, but the other part knows that it's probably not worth the trouble.

"Oh, here." I reach for the hot cocoa I sat on the table. "This is for you. Hopefully you like hot chocolate–it'll warm you up a bit."

When she takes it, her fingers brush against mine, and the moment our skin touches, our gazes lock. I probably imagine it, but it feels like a current of electricity rushes between us.

Looking down, her cheeks flame, turning a brilliant shade of pink.

"Thank you so much," Elizabeth breathes, still averting her eyes. "I should get going."

Clearing my throat, I nod. There's a part of me that's

disappointed that she doesn't seem to want to stay. There's an even bigger part of me that wants to ask her to.

"All right then," I say instead, swallowing down the desperate plea that wants to come out instead. I barely recognize myself right now. "Well, it was nice to meet you, letter for a name."

Look at me. Please, look at me.

For a moment I wonder if I said the words aloud, because she does, and we share a smile. Hesitantly, she starts to back away.

"It was nice to meet you too, last name for a first name."

Watching her go, I let my eyes rove over her body, and quickly realize she's about to trip again.

"Elizabeth! Careful!" I hiss, startling her into looking down where my gaze is cast. Her eyes widen as she realizes her mistake.

"Oh, my gosh." She slaps her forehead. "Thank you. It was nice to meet you!" she says in one breath, then turns around, giving me her back.

I watch her go, shouting out to her in my mind to turn back around, to look at me one last time, to come back and hang out with me on this cold December night.

Desperate fool, she doesn't even know you. You don't even know her.

But I want to. So badly, every bone in my body aches to be near her and I have no goddamn clue why.

My heart stutters when she glances back for a split

second before she walks out of the tent and back into the snowfall.

Sitting on top of the picnic table, I stare out into the dark, long past when she's out of sight. What are the odds that the one woman I've found myself attracted to in months happens to be passing through like a ship in the night?

She'll haunt my dreams until she's nothing more than a distant memory. A Christmas wish that didn't come true.

And a woman like that, I doubt I'll ever forget.

Zee

Chapter Eleven

"**S**weetheart, are you okay? You had us worried sick. You shouldn't be out in this weather!" Lincoln's mom rushes to the door the moment I push it open, wrapping me in a tight hug the second she sees me.

"I'm okay! I'm so sorry. I didn't mean to be gone so long." I hug her back, but don't tell her about my walk to the Christmas tree farm.

Lincoln comes through the kitchen alcove and pulls me from his mother's arms and into a hug of his own. Pressing his lips against my hair, he says loud enough for his mom to hear, "You had us worried," then he drops his voice, "I thought we had overwhelmed you, I know you were a little uncomfortable a couple times tonight, and I'm sorry for that. I'll admit the ruse has me feeling guilty too. I almost came clean while you were gone."

Looking up at him, I wrap my arms around his waist,

burying my nose into his sweater. Right now, he feels like an old friend rather than a practical stranger.

"Not at all. You and I are in this together. I guess you can call us besties now," I say, keeping my voice low so only he hears. Smiling at him, he looks at me and returns the gesture.

Part of me wishes I felt something deeper for him. My mind flashes with the image of Miller, and I'm surprised he's already infiltrated my thoughts. I had a feeling he would—I just thought it would be later, when I was alone in the dark, if you know what I mean.

Rubbing my arms, Lincoln declares, "Come on. You're freezing."

Not giving me time to take my snow gear off, Lincoln leads me into the living room, and we sit on the couch together around the fire.

"Up for another game?" Tim asks, tipping his head toward the stack of board games sitting on the coffee table.

I glance at my watch. "I'd love to, but just one. I think I want to get on the road within the next thirty minutes or so. It'll probably take me close to an hour and a half, if not a little longer, to get home. I don't want to rush it in these conditions, and I hurt my ankle on my walk, so I don't want to overdo it."

"You hurt your ankle?" Lincoln asks immediately. "Are you alright? Let me see it."

"I'm fine, I just rolled it. I sat for a few minutes to let it rest before I headed back."

"Which one?" His voice is strictly business.

Sighing, I relent. "My right."

Pulling my ankle into his lap, he unzips my boot and pulls it off.

"Holly! Your ankle is the size of a softball. How did you walk on this?"

"Er, carefully?" I laugh nervously, looking down at my ankle, which is, in fact, the size of a softball. "Honestly, it didn't even feel swollen."

"Probably because you're cold and in shock," he says in a chastising tone. I can tell by the way he's examining my ankle that he's in doctor mode. "Holly, we need to get some ice on this. Hey Mom, could you please get me an ice pack?" he yells at Tina, who's in the kitchen.

"Of course," she shouts, and a few seconds later she emerges with a bag of frozen peas in her hand. "Oh sweetheart, you walked on that? You must be in so much pain!"

"I'm fine, honestly. I didn't even feel it or know it was swollen until Lincoln pulled my boot off."

"I'm glad you said something," Lincoln's brow laced together, "but I really wish it hadn't happened. You shouldn't drive on this. I know that's not what you want to hear, but it's only going to make it worse."

Groaning, I cover my face with my hands, talking through my fingers, "I know, but I need to get back."

He looks at me with questions in his eyes as I lower my hands.

Lincoln doesn't know about my family or that I have no one to go home to.

Well, no one, except for Potato, and he'll be pissed if I don't make it back to feed him his wet food by morning.

"Sweetheart," Tina drawls. "Are you sure you won't just stay?"

"You can take my bedroom," Lincoln encourages. "I'll sleep on the couch."

Tim gives his son a sideways look at that suggestion, but thankfully keeps his comments to himself.

"I really can't stay," I stress. "I have to get home to my cat."

"You don't have a friend who can check on him?" A worry line creases Tina's forehead, and it sends a pang through my heart. Hesitating, I glance at the three sets of eyes on me.

"I mean..." I sigh. "Let me make a quick call."

Tina claps her hands together with excitement. "Yes! Call whomever you need to. Because you driving at night, in the snow, with *that*," she looks at my ankle, "is not safe. And I'd never forgive myself if you left and something happened to you."

"You're very sweet," I tell her. "Let me try to get ahold of my friend who lives in my building and see if she can keep an eye on Potato for me."

"Your cat's name is Potato?" Tim chuckles.

"You should see him! It'll make so much sense."

"I'd love for you to show us a picture when you're off the phone." He smiles, then waves his hand in my direction. "Go make your call."

"I will."

Hobbling down the hallway of the Stokes' home, I pull up my messages and send a text to Genesis, not really wanting to bother her on Christmas Eve, but grateful we exchanged keys shortly after becoming friends.

> Hey! I got stuck in Julian, hurt my ankle and can't drive home tonight. Would you mind feeding Potato his wet food in the morning? I'm so sorry to ask for a favor on Christmas.

Pressing my back against the wall, I slide down and sit on the floor, waiting to see if Gen texts back quickly. She has an addiction to technology and usually her responses come through immediately. I'm unsurprised to find that tonight is no different.

> Of course! Are you good? I could drive up and get you if you need me to?

> That's way too generous. I am fine, just going to spend the night at a friend's parents' house. I should be back by mid-morning.

> Sounds good, Zee, enjoy your night. Don't stress about Potato. He's in good hands.

> I know he is. Thank you so much for helping me.

Stowing my phone in my pocket, I use the wall to push myself to stand. When I go back into the living room, I meet Lincoln's eyes. "My friend is able to feed Potato. I'll stay."

"Good," Lincoln says with a nod. "Now let's get you off that ankle."

The next three hours go by full of laughter and fun as we play board games and sip eggnog while the fire roars. The snow has started up again, and from the large bay window in the living room, we're able to watch it fall gracefully. It's lovely, and for the first time since my family died, I feel at peace.

Somehow, the Stokes family went from being complete strangers to making me feel like one of their own in a matter of hours.

Later, when Tina declares it's time for her to go to bed, she pulls me in for a long hug when I stand, too. "I just want you to know," she whispers against my hair. "No matter what happens between you and my son, you always have a place here. I know you haven't opened up to us about your family, and I don't expect you to, but my motherly instincts tell me you have a story to tell—something you're not ready to talk about. When you're ready, I'm happy to listen. I know you don't know me from Adam, but I feel truly blessed to have you in my life now. Merry Christmas, Holly. Thanks for bringing me some peace of mind by staying here rather than brave the roads."

A tear streams down my face and I wipe it away as Tina and I part. She squeezes my shoulders and I give her a small smile, as much of one as I can muster when my heart feels like it's shattering.

I hate that I'm lying to her. It makes a part of my soul ache that I wasn't even aware existed.

It feels like *betrayal.*

"Well, I better get to bed too," Tim says with a yawn as he stretches his arms straight out. "G'night, you two." He winks at Lincoln, then follows his wife upstairs.

When we're alone, I sit in Tim's recliner.

"Look, Holly—" Lincoln says, at the same moment I say, "I think I'm going to—"

"I'm sorry." He laughs nervously, rubbing the back of his neck. "What were you going to say?"

"It's been a long day. I'm going to turn in too."

"Of course. Let me show you to the bedroom, and where the linens are. There's a bathroom just down the hall if you want to shower, and extra blankets in case you get cold."

"Thanks."

We stand in unison and he leads me up the stairs, pointing out the bathroom he mentioned and then showing me to his old bedroom.

Baseball memorabilia lines the walls, with old photos and knickknacks from his childhood. A full-sized bed sits in the center, and the room smells clean, like it's frequently tended to even though it's clear Lincoln doesn't live here.

"I thought your parents moved here after you moved

out?" I question, bending to look at an old photo of him when he was around nine or ten.

"They did, but my mom is a sucker for nostalgia. She decorated this room as best as she could from memory of my childhood bedroom, in case I was ever homesick."

"That's sweet." I check out the books sitting on the nightstand. Old classics, like *Call of the Wild* and *Catcher in the Rye.*

"That's my mom."

"You're lucky, you know."

"I know," he says softly. "Do you need anything?"

Slightly embarrassed, I turn to him and ask, "Got anything I can sleep in? An old shirt?"

"Of course. Top drawer. Want me to wash your sweater and jeans? At least they'd be clean by morning."

"You don't mind?"

"It's the least I can do."

"Okay, thanks. Give me a minute."

Nodding, Lincoln leaves the room and closes the door quietly behind him. Wasting no time, I open the top drawer of his dresser and pull out an old NASA T-shirt.

Stripping out of my clothes, I neatly fold my sweater, jeans, and socks, before tugging his T-shirt on. It hits just below my bottom, so I only crack the door when I thrust the clothes in his direction.

"They'll be waiting for you outside the door when you wake up," he says, respectfully keeping his eyes on mine as we speak through the crack.

"Thank you, Lincoln. For everything."

"Get some rest, Holly. There's ibuprofen in the bathroom if you need it for your ankle, and the door locks, if you feel more comfortable that way."

"I appreciate it. Goodnight."

"Goodnight."

The exchange feels awkward, like we've gone six steps backward since we met this morning.

Has it really not even been a full day since we met?

The thought is wild, but my mind doesn't give me much time to dwell on it, because the moment I sink between the comfortable down comforter and bamboo sheets of Lincoln's bedroom, my body immediately gets pulled into dreams of sugar plum fairies, and a ruggedly sexy man in plaid with a last name as a first name.

Zee

Chapter Twelve

A loud *bang* from the slamming of a car door rouses me from a restful sleep, and for a moment I forget I'm in a strange man's bed...*at his parents' house*. Sitting up, I stretch and yawn as the aroma of cinnamon rolls and coffee waft into my nose, and a smile graces my lips. It's Christmas morning, and while a devastating sense of sadness has embedded into my heart, the familiar feeling of excitement and wonder sits beside it, as though it's an old friend there to comfort.

Tossing the curtains open, a fresh blanket of sparkling white snow covers the ground, and from this angle I see a shiny red truck in the driveway that wasn't there before.

Muffled voices draw from downstairs, greetings and laughter, and I can't help but wonder who it is. Not that it's any of my business—I'm merely an overnight guest, but still, curiosity gets the better of me.

Cracking open the door, I'm happy to find my clothes

neatly folded and waiting for me on the ground, so I scoop them up, then close the door as quietly as I can. Seconds later, I'm redressed, slipping out of the bedroom. Tiptoeing to the bathroom, I close that door behind me, too.

Using my fingers, I try to manage my messy strands of hair and run my fingers under the water to clean up the makeup that smeared beneath my eyes. Pinching my cheeks, I attempt to add some color to them, wishing I was one of those girls who kept a small makeup bag in their purse. Finally, I look down at the counter, and am overjoyed to find a brand new toothbrush sitting next to the toothpaste.

Goodbye dragon breath.

When I'm ready to face the crowd downstairs, I give myself one more glance and know it's as good as it's going to get. The voices become louder as I start down the stairs, and I hear Tina saying, "Oh, I think Holly is awake." It sounds like she's in the living room, and when I round the corner, Lincoln meets me halfway.

"Good morning. Sleep well?" There's a cup of steaming hot coffee in his hands and I eye it, hoping there's more in the kitchen for me.

"I did, thank you. And thank you for washing my clothes last night. I appreciate it." I smile and glance down at the floor, pulling away from the heaviness of Lincoln's gaze.

Lincoln stares at me like he is waiting for something else, then smiles. "One tradition we have is our family gathers together on Christmas morning to open presents. Things have changed over the years, but my cousin still lives close by, so he's joining us this morning. I hope you don't mind."

"Of course not! I'm the one crashing your Christmas festivities."

"Not crashing, you were invited. Let me introduce you." He nods toward the living room. Placing his hand against my shoulder, he guides me around the corner.

Lincoln's cousin has his back to me, but Tina sees me immediately and smiles. Realizing her attention is elsewhere, Lincoln's cousin follows her line of sight, turning, and it's like everything happens in slow motion. I gasp, and the smile on his face drops as he takes me in, recognition immediately registering.

It's him.

Miller.

A single letter forms on his lips, and I know I have to stop him from saying my real name.

I can't believe I told him my real freaking name.

"Hi! I'm Holly, Holly North. Holly North! That's my name!" Rushing toward him, I extend my hand and hope the frantic plea in my eyes is enough for him to not question me.

Cocking his head to the side, his eyes narrow, but a smirk plays on his lips as he assesses me.

Taking my hand, he nods slowly.

"Holly, is it? I'm Miller. Miller Ryan." I can see the

questions floating through his mind, but to my relief, he doesn't ask them aloud.

"Nice to meet you!"

"Am I really that unmemorable?"

My heart plummets.

With his question, Lincoln's head snaps in his direction.

"What's that supposed to mean?" There's an edge in Lincoln's tone as he looks between me and his cousin.

"Last night, Holly here," he juts his thumb in my direction, "wandered down to the tree farm, and had her very own boxing match with my inventory." He turns to face me again. "How's that ankle?" I'm surprised to see concern swimming in his gorgeous brown eyes.

Through gritted-teeth, I steal a glance at Lincoln, then turn back to Miller. "Much better. Thank you again for the ice."

"So that's where you ended up last night?" Lincoln questions, his lips turning down in a frown. Crossing his arms over his chest, he eyes Miller, shaking his head.

I wish I could read his thoughts.

"Oh, at least she was in good hands!" Tina chimes in. Whether she notices the tension in the room, she doesn't say, but her timing feels intentional. Like she's providing back up, saving me from the shade these two are throwing at each other.

Knowing I need to fix this, I turn my focus to Lincoln.

But not before realizing Miller's still holding my hand in his.

Dropping it, I step away. "Yes," I explain. "I saw a tree farm on my way here yesterday, and when I started to walk, my subconscious took me back there. And because I am, well, me, I ended up tripping over an extension cord. That's how I hurt my ankle."

"Understatement of the century," Miller mutters under his breath, and Lincoln's gaze snaps back to him.

"Elaborate," Lincoln says flatly.

"What Holly's left out of her story is when she tripped, she took five and a half trees down with her."

"I did not take five and a half trees down with me. How do you take down *half* a tree?" Crossing my arms defiantly, I glare at him, which only makes him grin wider.

"I caught it, remember?"

I let out an annoyed huff, then toss my hands into the air. "All right, there you have it, Stokes family. Holly North is a giant klutz." I laugh, but it comes out a little manically.

Because if you can't laugh at yourself, then how can you handle when other people laugh at you?

Suddenly, I'm fighting back tears. Looking up at the ceiling, I blink several times, desperate to not let them fall.

"Holly, can I get you a cup of coffee?" Tim holds up his own cup and gives it a little shake. "I'm about to refill mine."

"That would be amazing, thank you."

"How do you take it?"

"A little coffee and a lot of creamer, please."

He chuckles, then heads to the kitchen.

"So, Holly, I'm not sure if Lincoln has filled you in, but

one family tradition we have is to open presents on Christmas morning, then we have a light breakfast. This year I made homemade cinnamon rolls. How does that sound?" Tina loops her arm through mine and guides me over to the couch where a stack of presents sits neatly wrapped in brown gift paper with sparkly red and green bows.

My eyes widen at the sight. "This isn't for me, is it?"

"Of course it is!" Tina looks at me like I've grown another head. "Now, we didn't know too much about you, but being a woman myself, I was able to make some educated decisions about what you might like."

"This is far too generous." A fresh swell of tears lines my bottom lashes, and I suck in my bottom lip to keep from having a complete breakdown.

"Nonsense!" She picks up one of the smaller gifts from the top of the pile and thrusts it into my hands.

"I brought gifts as well, but nothing like this. I can't believe you did this for me." I feel awestruck and like my gifts are insignificant. They're just trinkets from the gift area at my work. Nothing special. Nothing like the mountain of gifts sitting in front of me.

"Holly, trust me, it's not so much for you as it is for her." Tim extends my coffee cup, laughing. "Tina has a bit of a shopping problem."

She smacks her husband against the chest with the back of her hand. "Oh, you shush!"

Wrapping his arm around her, he pulls her close and kisses the top of her head.

From across the room, Miller watches the exchange with fascination, his eyes never leaving mine for long, despite being engaged deep in conversation with his cousin.

Lincoln's back is to me, but by the way Miller occasionally nods his head, I assume Lincoln is trying to sell him the story of me being his holidate.

I can't believe this is happening.

"Come, sit boys," Tina singsongs, patting the couch next to her.

Both men look at each other one last time, seemingly communicating without words, then they cross the room. Miller takes the spot where Tina's hand just was, and Lincoln comes to sit by me.

"Alright," she continues. "Just like when you were little! Have at it."

Lincoln leans over and whispers, "That essentially means it's a free-for-all. Go ahead and open your presents." My breath catches in my throat when he presses a kiss to the side of my head before straightening and taking a gift from his pile.

From my peripheral, Miller stiffens.

Looking up at Lincoln, I nod, trying to push the lump from my throat. My heart's hammering in my chest—so scared that Miller is going to out me at any second, and Lincoln and I will have to do some serious damage control.

Although part of me already suspects that Tina knows this relationship is fabricated.

There's another weight sitting on my chest—the one that doesn't want to hurt Miller.

Which is *crazy*. I don't even know him! But I want to. A flicker of something ignited in me last night, and I have a never-ending freefall of questions zinging through my mind, along with an undeniable attraction to him.

Ten minutes later, all the presents are open. Scattered around the floor and furniture is the discarded wrapping paper and bows, and a heaping pile of goodies sitting in front of each of us.

"I'm sorry I didn't know you would be here, *Holly*, or I would have brought you something." Miller leans back against the couch, extending his denim covered legs wide in a relaxed position. Lifting his arms, he clasps his hands behind his head and tries not to smile.

"I wasn't supposed to stay. But my ankle would have made it very difficult to drive back to the city."

"You live in San Diego?"

I nod. "On the outskirts."

He says nothing, but I can practically see the cogs of his mind working as he watches me like a predator watches their prey.

"Nice to see you were able to spend the night." Miller turns to Lincoln. "It's been a while since you've been up here."

"The hospital's been demanding, but I was just here for Thanksgiving. Or have you forgotten already?"

"Haven't forgotten. How could I?"

My head volleys, following them as they converse. It's

clear there's some sort of tension between them, and I'm very curious what it is.

Is it me? Am I the problem causing strife between them?

Not everything's about you, Zee.

Tina sighs dramatically, then goes into the kitchen without saying a word. Tim grabs ahold of the remote and turns on the TV, choosing to ignore the squabble that is happening right across from him.

But I can't look away. Which proves to be dangerous when both men turn their attention to me at the same time.

"Holly, can I get a word alone?" they say in unison, word for word, serious expression for serious expression. As they turn to each other with scowls, a horrifying panic strikes me in the center of my chest.

Knowing my loyalty needs to be with Lincoln, seeing as I'm his fake-girlfriend and all, I stand when he does, and follow him from the room.

He's silent as he leads me to the back porch and closes the door behind us. Without my jacket, I immediately begin to shiver.

"Did something happen between you and my cousin last night?" Lincoln doesn't waste time beating around the bush. His voice is practically a bark, but surprisingly doesn't hold an accusation within his question. His gaze softens slightly when he sees the surprise written all over my face, especially when my jaw slackens.

"I...what? Seriously? I wasn't even gone long enough

for anything to happen! I tripped and fell. He got me ice for my ankle. I waited a few minutes until it felt okay to walk on, then I came back. End of story."

"Holly, I have no claim over you." His voice is low and silky. "If something happened between you two, I'm not upset. I just need to know so we can get our stories straight."

"Why does it matter? I'm going to be leaving in a few minutes anyway, and then none of you will ever have to see me again." *Great, that just made me sound guilty, when I haven't done anything wrong.*

"It matters because I know Miller better than I know myself."

"Okay?"

Rubbing my hands up and down my arms, I try to bring some warmth back to my body, and eye the back door. Why do we have to do this outside? Where it's freezing? And where my jacket isn't?

"I haven't seen him look at a woman like he looked at you since we were teenagers."

"What's that supposed to mean, Lincoln? Stop talking in riddles because I'm not going to figure it out. Not when my body's shutting down from hypothermia."

"He wants you, Holly."

A nervous laugh rumbles from my lips. "Oh my gosh, you have got to be kidding me! We spent maybe ten minutes together last night, half of which I was lying on the ground in utter embarrassment. And the other half was with ice on my ankle! You're insane if you think he wants me."

"No, I know I'm correct. Look, I'm under no illusion that you're my girlfriend. Obviously, this is just for show, and while I truly appreciate what you've done, I also know when I am being friend-zoned. You friend-zoned me from the moment we met at that coffee shop. Which is completely fine, I'm not interested in being anything other than friends, but now Miller is involved. And I think he's interested in you. I'd put money on it."

"I don't even know him. We met for ten minutes," I repeat as a shiver overtakes my body. Lincoln steps forward and rubs his hands against my arms.

"I know. But I can tell by the look on your face that *you're* interested in him, too."

"Oh, Jesus. I'm here with you. And your audacity is quite large, my *friend*."

Lincoln laughs, but ignores me and continues singing his cousin's praises. "Miller is a standup guy. Loyal, family oriented. He's also incredibly selfless, and these last several years, his family has needed him. And he's put them first."

Am I on a secret dating show right now? What the heck is happening? "Why are you telling me all this, Lincoln?"

"Because in the last twenty-four-ish hours of getting to know you, I've learned you are the type of woman I'd want to bring home to my mother."

A nervous giggle erupts from me. "Didn't you?"

"Yes, but maybe this is bigger than the two of us. Maybe I didn't bring you home for me."

A pregnant pause lies between us. Through the small window in the porch door, we see Miller standing at the kitchen counter, talking to his aunt. They're smiling and laughing, and as she reaches up to his face, for some reason, I envision them as younger versions of themselves, and I feel like I'm encroaching on a memory.

"This is a lot. I've literally only known you and your family for one day."

"I'm not trying to creep you out."

"Well, you are. This is way too much. You literally brought me to help you, and now I feel like I'm being sold off to your cousin."

He laughs, shaking his head wildly. "God, no, Holly! That's not at all what I'm trying to do."

It's what it feels like, buddy.

Glancing at my watch, I use the time as a method of escape. "Look, I should probably get on the road."

Truth be told, everything feels awkward. A little unsettling.

"At least have breakfast first, and a cup of coffee." He tips his head at the coffee cup in my hand that I haven't touched yet. It's no longer steaming.

"I'm in the *Twilight Zone*," I murmur.

"I'm so sorry. I can tell I've made you uncomfortable. That's not my intention. All I wanted you to know was that if there *is* something, some sort of spark, or even just a physical attraction with my cousin, there will be no hard feelings."

"And with your family? How on earth would we explain that?"

Lincoln shrugs. "I guess we would just need to come clean."

"They'd hate me. Not to mention this is *so* hypothetical it isn't even funny."

"I know. Let's just go inside and have some breakfast, then you can get on the road. Trust me, you don't want to miss my mom's famous cinnamon rolls. They're just as good, if not better, as that Julian caramel apple pie we had last night." He playfully pokes his elbow into the side of my ribs.

"I don't know," I muse sarcastically. "I believe you, but that apple pie was something else. I'm kind of sad all the shops will be closed, and that I can't take one home."

"I'm staying up here another day—I found coverage for my shift. Do you want me to bring you one when I get back into the city?"

For a split second, I contemplate his offer. The pie was *that* good. "No, that's nice of you to offer though."

"Well, you know how to reach me if you change your mind. It's the least I can do." Moving to the door, Lincoln opens it and gestures for me to walk in front of him.

The moment I step through the doorway, my eyes connect with Miller's, and my heart shudders. Blowing out a shaky breath, I remind myself that I'm here to be Lincoln's girlfriend. The ruse is almost finished. The only thing standing between me and a successful last holidate is a pastry.

I can do this.

Though the way Miller is looking at me is making my insides as gooey as a cinnamon roll.

Miller

Chapter Thirteen

Well, if this isn't the most awkward thing to happen to me in God knows how long. Sitting at my aunt and uncle's kitchen table, we all eat in deafening silence. Them, me, Lincoln, and *Elizabeth*.

Taking another bite of the cinnamon deliciousness my aunt has crafted, I observe Linc and Zee. Watching them closely, it doesn't take a rocket scientist to know something isn't right between them.

I can sense it.

There's no chemistry. Their actions feel forced, like they are strictly friends, but are pretending to be more for the sake of Linc's parents.

They *have* been desperate for him to settle down—they've been on me about it, too—is it possible Little Linc has asked a friend to step in and *pretend* to be his girlfriend?

There's no damn way.

When everyone's finished with their breakfast, and the plates have been cleared, Zee heads toward the coatrack and pulls off her jacket, swinging it out so she can slip her arms through the sleeve. It's obvious she's about to leave, and I know this is my opportunity.

"Holly, could we talk for a second?" Calling her a fake name feels like acid on my tongue. My heart stops, knowing there's a very real possibility she'll say no.

Peering up at me from under her lashes, she agrees. "Sure."

It feels like my heart can beat again.

Opening the front door, I nod for her to go out in front of me. She looks behind us to see if anyone is watching, then heads outside.

As soon as the door is closed, I take a step closer to her. "What's with the fake name?"

Lifting her chin, she narrows her eyes. "How do you know it isn't my real name?"

"Pretty uncommon to introduce yourself as your nickname, then explain your full name, if it's not real." I take another step forward.

"Maybe." She licks her lips, and my eyes drop to her mouth for a moment.

"I don't buy it," I counter, regaining my focus. "Holly is just too much of a *Holly Jolly* name for it to be real. What's your last name, again?"

"North," she says without a shred of hesitation.

Barking a laugh, I look at her like she has to be joking, but she just stares at me like a deer in the headlights.

"Holly North? *That's* the best you could come up with? How did my aunt and uncle not see right through it? How did *Linc* not see right through it?"

Shaking my head, I rub my palms up and down my face in disbelief as more laughter erupts from my chest.

"Did you want something?" Her arms cross in front of her with annoyance. There's fire in her eyes.

It makes my dick hard. She's so damn beautiful, and from what I'm gathering, has a streak of humor, too.

"I *do*, actually." Taking another step closer, she takes one back, the pull to my push. Her back hits the railing of the porch, and I place my fists against the snow-covered wood, ignoring the cold bite as I cage her in.

Refusing to let her look away, I hold her gaze. "Are you *actually* dating my cousin?"

A flush creeps up her neck from beneath where the collar of her jacket exposes it, settling against her cheeks. "Ye—yes," she stammers, but it's not hard to tell she's lying to me.

Leaning in, I level my mouth with her ear. "I'm not a fan of liars, Elizabeth." Then I push myself from the railing, taking a step back to give her space.

There's a war raging in her brain. I can tell by the various looks that wash over her features, but I wait patiently, letting her figure out what it is she wants to say to me.

It's amusing, really, and I can't fight the smile I feel tugging at my lips.

Finally, I watch as frustration settles as the most potent

emotion, and she pinches the bridge of her nose. "Okay! I'm not actually dating Lincoln. He asked me to be his date for Christmas Eve because Tina and Tim have been pestering him about settling down."

"What's in it for you?" The question springs from my lips, coming out more accusatory than I intended.

"Nothing," she snaps.

"You're lying again."

"God, are you always this irritating?"

"Only on days that end with y."

She's pissed, and it's adorable, especially now that the tip of her nose has turned rosy from the cold.

"There's nothing in it for me." She stares down at the ground, her voice a mere whisper in the wind, but I am able to hear her with no problem. My body and mind feel so in tune with this woman, it's catching me off guard.

I've never been a man who believes in love at first sight, or soulmates, but Holly, er, Elizabeth has me rethinking things.

When she looks up at me again, her eyes flick to the front door, then she takes a step forward, closing some of the distance I put between us. Her voice is low when she says, "I lost my family not that long ago, and the idea of spending Christmas alone felt like a knife to the gut. So here I am."

A knife to the gut. I can understand that feeling, because it's currently settled in me after hearing her say that. "I'm sorry." My fingers itch to reach out and touch her, but I don't. It feels too vulnerable.

I also remind myself she's a complete stranger.

"I should get on the road. I don't wanna take up anymore of your family's Christmas, and I need to get back to my cat."

Moving a step around me, she reaches for the doorknob.

"Wait," I blurt. Reaching up, I rub the back of my neck, looking down at the ground, before meeting her gaze again. "Can I get your phone number?"

Can I get your phone number? Why do I have to sound like I'm a timid eighth grader?

All I know is I can't let her get away again.

Her brows knit together. "You want my phone number?"

"Yeah, Elizabeth. I do."

Then she does something I haven't seen since last night, and it makes the damn fluttering in my gut happen again.

She smiles.

Zee

Chapter Fourteen

"Are you sure you can't stay longer? Christmas dinner will be at about two," Tina tries to persuade as she hugs me tight, gripping the back of my shoulders in her embrace.

"I really can't stay, Tina. But thank you for the invitation. Yesterday and this morning were wonderful."

When she releases me, I fight against tears. This goodbye feels bittersweet—like when you drop a loved one off at the airport, unsure of when the next visit will be. It hurts, but you'll carry the memories from your time with them until you see them again.

Tina's hand drops to mine, and she squeezes it in a motherly way as she smiles at me, obviously attempting to cheer me up.

"Well, kiddo, it was so nice to meet you." Tim pushes his way past his wife and envelops me into a giant bear hug. His arms are warm as he gives me a squeeze, then, as he steps back, the cold threatens to swallow me whole.

I shiver and turn to Lincoln, who's standing just a few steps away, watching me say goodbye to his parents.

"Thank you again," I tell them, swiping away a tear. "For everything. Truly."

Lincoln puts his arm around me and guides me to the car. He opens my door, then turns our bodies so his back is to his family, concealing me from view. Leaning down, he speaks by my ear, so it looks like we're sharing a kiss.

"I owe you one, Holly North."

"No, you don't. Thank you for sharing your family with me. Even if it was under false pretenses, it's because of you all that I actually got to enjoy the holiday."

He gives me a weak smile, knowing I won't say more. Nodding, he brings me to his chest and hugs me tight. "Get home safe, and please, let's stay in contact. I'd really like to be your friend."

A sob lodges in my throat, but I try to hold myself together. My voice is small as I choke out, "I will," then pull away from his arms and sink into my driver's seat.

Lincoln closes my door for me, and I crank the key in the ignition, turning the heater on full blast as the engine comes to life.

The tears start to fall before I've even made it back to the main road. As I pull away from the Stokes' house, my heart feels like there's a brick tied around it.

Glancing in the rearview mirror, I see Tim and Tina

watching me leave as they hold each other around the waist. Lincoln and Miller seem to be arguing about something on the porch—Lincoln gestures toward my car, but I have to force myself to pry my eyes away and refocus on the road as Miller's gaze follows Lincoln's outstretched hand.

This is so stupid. They're *not* my family.

But it almost feels as though in the last twenty-four hours I've become a part of theirs.

I'm delusional, I think to myself.

With the GPS secured on my dashboard screen, I grab my cell phone and pull up Genesis' number while keeping my eye on the road.

"Hey!" she answers on the second ring. "Merry Christmas."

"Merry Christmas, Gen!" My tone is brighter than I'm feeling, especially when I pass by the Ryan Family Tree Farm. My heart sinks and lodges in my throat, which doesn't even make sense. "How's Potato?"

"He was just fine. Didn't even come out of the room until I went to find him, then he realized I was there to feed him."

"Sounds about right." I make a right-hand turn onto the main road, and it immediately winds me out of town.

"His collar is *so* cute! You're lucky it wouldn't fit on Pebbles or I would have stolen it." Pebbles is her Great Dane, and possibly the laziest dog I've ever met. If Potato didn't hate other animals, I bet they'd be two peas in a pod.

"You could try! It'd probably fit her. Potato has a big ol' neck."

"Wait, Potato has a neck? I couldn't tell. He looks like one big ball of fluff."

We're both laughing, which helps pull me from my sadness a little, but I'm still not really in the mood for chitchat, so I opt to end the call. "Hey, listen. I'm on my way home, but I wanted to check in. The roads are super icy, though, so I should probably hang up. Thanks again for feeding him this morning. Do you work this week? We can catch up then?"

"You made the schedule, Zee! I'll see you tomorrow, and you know I'm always happy to help with Potato. Drive carefully!"

My finger hovers over the 'End Call' button on my dash screen as I tell her, "Thank you, see you then." Ending the call, the Christmas music returns through my speakers with the lovely sound of the group, Pentatonix.

I'm obsessed with them, so I turn it up and start singing along.

The roads are clear, so the drive is relatively easy— hardly any other cars pass me—so imagine my surprise when, from my rearview mirror, I see a truck come barreling around a turn.

For the second time in twenty minutes, my heart sinks. Gripping the steering wheel like a granny, I keep my eyes firmly on the road while holding my breath, waiting for the inevitable moment where the driver crosses into the other lane and blows past me.

But it doesn't happen.

Looking into my rearview mirror, I find the truck entirely too close for comfort.

Then I see the driver.

"Oh, hell!" What's Miller doing?

Speeding up, I put some distance between our vehicles, but he quickly closes it.

This freaking guy.

He signals for me to pull over, but I ignore him and return my attention to the road, driving another couple of miles before looking into my mirror again.

When I do, he gives me the same signal.

Up ahead, I see a turn out, so I let off the gas and activate my turn signal before guiding my car off the road.

Unsurprisingly, Miller does the same.

Turning my car off, I yank the keys from the ignition and toss open my door. As I step out of the vehicle, Miller gets out of his and starts toward me.

"What are you doing?" My voice is shaking, but I'm not scared. I'm annoyed.

It's freaking cold out here, and I shiver, having shrugged out of my jacket when I cranked the heater before leaving the Stokes'.

Miller doesn't look cold, though. His black and red flannel looks warm and cozy, and he seems unphased as he smirks. "Following you home."

"What? Why would you do that?"

"Because I'm not going to let you spend Christmas alone, Elizabeth."

"How do you know I'm spending it alone?" My breath catches.

"Are you?"

Kicking a lump of snow, I look down at the ground. "Yes."

Miller takes a couple of steps closer to me. "Well, you're not anymore."

Meeting his gaze, I search for the catch. The angle. The *game* he's obviously playing.

"Why do you care?" I try to give him an attitude to mask the wild beating of my heart that's making me want to spring into tears.

A car zooms past, startling me, and I gasp. Miller takes another step closer, positioning himself between me and the road.

"I don't know. But I do," he says with a husky voice, his eyes dipping to my mouth. Without thinking, I lick my lips.

"You shouldn't. Go back to your family, Miller."

"No."

"Why not?"

He takes another step closer until we're toe to toe. Inside of my chest, my heart hammers so violently, I'm convinced he can hear it.

Reaching his hand up, he tangles it in my hair, cupping the base of my head. "I'm exactly where I want to be." The air grows thick around us, hard to breathe, despite being outside. Then, the world stands still when he asks, "Can I kiss you?"

Inhaling, words swirl through my mind, but nothing forms as a response. I forget how to speak, all sense of the English language gone out the window.

His other hand floats up to the side of my cheek, his knuckles brushing against my skin. "Elizabeth, can I kiss you?" he repeats, his voice as strangled as my heart feels.

My brain is screaming *yes*, but instead of a three letter, single syllable word, I somehow end up saying, "Why would you want to kiss me?"

"Why do you ask so many questions?" He brushes his thumb over my bottom lip, and a rush of arousal flashes through me, warming my core. "This time, give me an answer. Yes or no?"

"Yes."

There's a moment before every kiss where a woman's heart seems to do acrobatics in her chest, flip-flopping with excitement as the anticipation builds right before it happens. Right now is no different. The way Miller looks at me sends my heart ice-skating around my chest. His smile sends shockwaves through my system in little bouts of tingles radiating through each nerve.

I want to pull him close and push him away.

Then his lips are on mine.

The kiss starts slow at first, the warmth of his skin penetrates the coldness of mine, and I feel him smile against me before his lips begin to move, coaxing my mouth to open and allow him access.

Naturally, my arms lift to wrap around his neck, and he takes that opportunity to pull me closer, moving one arm around my waist while the other stays firmly in my hair.

Melting in his arms, I let him take full control as our tongues meet, but the moment they do, he pulls away.

His eyes have darkened, yet still sparkle as he slowly releases me. "Well, damn."

I want more—I want his mouth on mine again.

But then another car speeds by and reminds me we're literally standing on the side of the road.

Stupidly, I breathe, "So now that you've gotten your kiss, are you going back home?"

Why must you open your mouth, Zee?

Miller laughs and kisses my forehead. "Not a chance, Snow Angel. Come on, get back in the car and let's get you warm again."

Funny, I don't feel cold anymore.

"Okay," I agree pliantly, letting him steer me back to my driver's side door. "Then what?"

Wow, how did one kiss render me completely stupid?

"Then you'll give me your address in case we get separated, and I'll follow you home for Christmas."

"You're actually coming back with me?"

"I told you I was." Miller smiles with that same lopsided smile and I'm pretty sure I melt into a pile of goo against my fabric seats.

Bending at the waist, he reaches in and grabs ahold of my seatbelt, buckling it for me.

"Text it to me," he commands, knocking on the top of my car twice before stepping away.

"I don't have your number."

"Yes, you do. I texted it to you before we got out."

Backing away, he watches me the entire time until he makes it back to his truck. Shutting my car door, I grab my phone and look at it, seeing that he did, in fact, send me a message.

Hi

Typing my address quickly, I press send, then toss the phone onto the seat next to me, like it will physically hurt me if I don't get it out of my hand.

Blowing out a shaky breath, I turn the key, letting the engine roar to life.

It's going to be a long way home knowing the lumber snack is following me.

I wonder what Potato will think.

Zee

Chapter Fifteen

The keys rattle in my hand as I try to fit the big gold one into the lock, my palm so slick with sweat there's a hundred percent possibility I'll drop them before figuring out how to open the door.

Standing behind me, Miller crowds my space, his fingertips ghosting down my spine, as he waits patiently. He's making it even harder to think than it already is.

When I finally wrestle with the door, I push it so forcefully I trip through the threshold and stumble inside.

"Welcome to my humble abode." On the outside I'm cool as a cucumber, but deep down the nerves have me feeling nauseous.

Miller lets out a low whistle as he walks in, shutting the door behind him as he looks around. "Very homey. It's nice. Not exactly what I envisioned for you, though."

"What exactly did you envision?"

"Something a little quirkier. Bright colors, strange knickknacks."

"Well, sorry that my neutral color palette isn't what you had in mind. I do love some pops of color though." I gesture to the couch, where my bright green throw blanket rests over the top of it, and my red Christmas pillows adorn the cushions. "See?"

"Very merry." A smile plays on his lips.

Tossing my keys down on my entryway table, I shrug out of my jacket, and lay it on the back of the dining chair.

My apartment is small and modest. An open floor plan, except for the bedroom and bathroom. Perfect for just me.

Well, me and Potato.

Speaking of...

"Potato," I call out. "Pstpstpst."

Miller laughs boisterously, and I frown in confusion. "What?"

"What was that noise?"

"What noise?"

"The noise you just made."

"What? The pstpstpst?"

"Yeah." He laughs again.

Rolling my eyes playfully, I tell him, "The universal cat call. You've never heard it?"

"Nope. The only cat calls I know are the sleazy ones."

"Not a cat person?"

This is a pivotal moment. If he's not a cat person, it'll tell me everything I need to know about him.

Please be a cat person. Please be a cat person.

"I'm not *not* a cat person, I've just only ever had dogs. My parents aren't cat people, though. They're not a fan of the litter boxes."

"That's what self-cleaning ones are for," I scoff, mildly offended that people—not just Miller's parents, but all people who do—let something as trivial as where a cat does their business prevent them from getting a cat. "You haven't had pets of your own?"

"Just the ones on the farm."

"Would you like something to drink?" Preemptively, I go into the kitchen and pull out two mugs.

"What are my choices?"

"Well, it's Christmas. So eggnog, cider, hot cocoa, coffee, or the regular beverage options like water, milk, etcetera."

"I'll have whatever you're having."

"Coffee it is." Firing up my coffee maker, it gurgles to life with the click of a button, then I busy myself, gathering the other ingredients in order to make a latte at home. Sneaking glances at Miller, I observe as he takes in my apartment, giving everything his full attention before he looks at something else. It's like he's getting to know me by examining the items around him. It makes me feel a little anxious. "So tell me about these animals."

"Well, I do actually have a cat, but he's a barn cat, so not much of a pet."

He does *have a cat!*

"What's his name?"

"Er—" He purses his lips. "Barn Cat?"

"Seriously, Miller!" I scold. "Your cat needs a proper name!"

"Well, maybe when you meet him, you can name him for me."

Heat rises up my cheeks, and I bite my lip. "You want me to meet your cat?"

He shrugs, but a dimple forms when he tries to suppress his smile. "I think you two would get along."

"What other animals do you have?"

"Penny, my border collie. Plus a horse, two cows, four goats, and a hoard of chickens."

"Do they have names?"

"Must everything have a name?"

Looking at him with a wide-eyed sarcastic expression, I nod.

Dramatically, Miller sighs, then relents. "The horse is Palmer, and the cows are Chocolate, and Strawberry. The goats and chickens don't have names, except pain in my ass one, pain in my ass two, you get the picture."

"I want to meet them all."

"You will. Now, where is this cat of yours? You've held me in suspense for long enough."

"Let me go find him. He's probably lounging some-where, ignoring us. Make yourself comfortable."

Miller pulls out one of the kitchen chairs and sinks into it, slouching slightly as he spreads his legs, looking as relaxed as can be. He looks like he's been here a thousand times, and that pulls at something in my heart.

Walking into my bedroom, I push the door open further, and immediately see Potato spread out on my bed, laying in the sliver of sun that warms my blanket. He doesn't bother opening his eyes until I sit on the bed next to him, forcing him to see who has interrupted his nap.

Scratching behind his ears, I press a kiss onto his nose. "Rise and shine, sleepyhead, I have someone I want you to meet."

Scooping him into my arms, his side lays against my chest while I hold him belly up. As we walk, it bounces and sways in time with the red jingle bell hanging from his collar. The cute little Christmas tree and gingerbread man hanging from it swing with each step, too.

Potato's face is scrunched in a smooshy-faced frown, and I can tell he's annoyed by the way I am holding him like a baby, but that's exactly what he is.

My furry baby.

Cue the social media "I just a baby" sound in my head.

Miller stands as I enter the room, and as I pass by the light switch, I flip on the Christmas lights that decorate my living room area, making my quaint little space more merry and bright.

As Potato and I grow closer, Miller's eyes widen when he sees him, and he meets me halfway, letting out a guttural laugh. "Wow, he's so…"

"Adorable? Handsome? He loves his compliments— better lay it on thick."

"Uh, I was going to say large. But handsome works too."

My cat gives a grumpy little meow.

"You've got one paw that's lighter than the other, huh, buddy?" Miller tries to baby talk, taking Potato's lighter paw between two fingers.

Potato meows again, but this time it's a little more high-pitched—his way of saying to stop holding his paw, I assume.

It's obvious that Miller hasn't spent a lot of time around cats, because I can't help but laugh as he reaches out and pets the top of Potato's head like you would pet a dog. His strokes are rough, and Potato's ears immediately flatten as Miller unknowingly smashes his head further and further into his neck as he tries to retract it with each pet.

I'm laughing so hard I can't breathe.

Potato isn't amused, though, and struggles to get in an upright position, leaping from my arms and running into my bedroom again.

I'm not sure I've seen him run so fast in the entire time I've had him.

"Is it a deal breaker if the cat doesn't like me?" Miller laughs, but rubs the back of his neck, looking a little nervous.

"I won't call it a deal breaker, yet, but you need to do your best to win him over. Him and I are a package deal."

"Noted."

I touch his chest before I go back into the kitchen to

finish making our cups of coffee. When they're ready, I hand him a steaming mug.

The scent of coffee and peppermint permeates the air as I bring mine to my lips and take a small sip so as not to burn my tongue. "You said you wanted what I was having. I hope a peppermint mocha is okay."

"Sure." Miller takes a tentative sip, and I can tell by the face he tries to hide that it's not his favorite.

"Too sweet?"

"Sweeter than I normally take my coffee, but it's good. Thank you." This time, when he brings the cup back to his lips, he takes a long gulp. *That has to hurt.*

"So, I wasn't prepared to have a guest for Christmas. I don't have any of the fixings for a typical Christmas dinner."

"What was your original plan for today?"

"Honestly?"

"Of course."

"To take a long shower, put on my coziest, albeit frumpiest, pajamas, and order Chinese takeout."

"Oh, so you're a Christmas takeout kind of girl?"

"Not normally. But this year..." my voice trails off, and I shrug, looking down into my cup.

Miller covers my hand with his and shifts them until he's able to lace our fingers together. "Do you want to talk about it?"

I shake my head. "We're practically strangers. I don't need to trauma dump on you."

Miller winces, and I immediately regret my word

choice. "Look, Zee, I know we just met, but it doesn't feel like it. It feels different. At least for me."

"Different how?"

"Like I've been waiting my whole life to meet you."

We hold each other's gaze, and there's a part of my subconscious that realizes this should be weird. This *should* feel off. I barely know this man, yet here he is, standing in my kitchen on Christmas Day less than twenty-four hours after the world's most embarrassing introduction.

"I say we stick to your original plan," he says, breaking the short silence. "Christmas movies, you take your shower, we eat Chinese."

"That's it? What's the catch? Isn't this the part where you should be trying to seduce me, or in a different plot twist, the part where you kidnap me and harvest my organs?"

"Last time I checked, it was Christmas, not Halloween, so no harvesting of any organs this year. Maybe next." His dimple returns, and he pushes a lock of hair behind my ear. "As for the seduction, as much as I want to find out if you taste like Christmas, I like you too much to rush this past any point you are comfortable with. I meant what I said, Elizabeth. It feels like I've been waiting my whole life to meet you. I'm not the type of man who goes to bars, or clubs, or swipes through dating apps."

I bite my tongue, guilt flickering through me as he mentions the dating apps. But that's not *typically* me, either. I only reactivated my profile to set up some holiday dates. Aside from those, I was never active on the site.

"My life revolves around my family and my work. Julian's a small town, and as much as I love San Diego, it's not a priority to come down the mountain often enough to meet someone. Believing in fate has never been my thing, but it seems a little coincidental that you *quite literally* tripped and fell into my lap last night. I don't know what that means, but I don't want to take it for granted. I want to get to know you. I want you to know me."

My heart soars as I stare into his shimmering brown eyes, unable to formulate words after his declaration of interest. It's something a man hasn't expressed to me in ages, aside from the flattery I received in SparksFly messages, but those were only surface deep.

This is something else entirely.

So, of course, I do what any sane woman in my position would do. I jump into his arms, forcing him to catch me as I smash my lips into his.

Sinking into the kiss, I melt against him as he rests both of his large palms on my butt, holding me to him as he meets me with equal ferocity. A whimper vibrates through my throat, encouraging Miller to deepen it.

Walking with me in his arms, Miller attempts to navigate his way through my small apartment, yet still manages to bump into the side of the kitchen table and the back of the couch as he leads us to the living room. I'm brought down into his lap as he sinks into the soft cushions, and my fingers curl into the hair at the nape of his neck, pulling him closer to me as we kiss like we're teenagers, desperate for each other.

"Are you sure this is what you want?" Miller asks against my lips, playing with the hem of my sweater.

"Yes. Are you?"

"I don't think I've ever wanted anything more, Snow Angel. It's too bad there's not a bow on you because you're my gift this year." Pulling my sweater over my head, he tosses it to the side. My lacy cream bra accentuates my breasts, which are at eye level for him now, and he sucks in a breath.

"Wait a second." I giggle, then slide off his lap. My bare feet feel cool against the floor as I back away from Miller, wondering if I can pull this off. He gives me a pouty face as I walk into my bedroom and the moment I'm out of his line of sight, I spin and run to my closet.

Pushing the heavy wood sliding door, I pull down the unused box of gift wrap and search for the red ribbon I know I have stashed inside. Pulling it out, I grab the scissors too, then cut off a long piece. The satin feels soft in my hand, the shiny, deep crimson malleable as I tie it around my waist in a bow.

It doesn't look as cute as I envisioned in my head, but it'll do.

Unbuttoning my jeans, I push them down my legs and kick out of them. With a quick swish of my hand against my skin, I realize they're a little stubbly, but it's too late to shave now.

It's not like I planned this. Thank God I did shave yesterday morning at least, or he'd have an entire forest to deal with.

Banishing my nerves, I fluff my hair and arrange it so it lays partially over my shoulder, then I reach up and pinch my cheeks, hoping to add some color. Emerging from my bedroom, I sashay my hips back as I walk in, and Miller immediately follows me with his gaze. His eyes darken as he takes in my mismatched bra and panties, and the bow I've wrapped myself in.

He says nothing, and with every step closer I take, and the lingering silence, I become more unsure of my actions. Miller's features harden slightly as I stop right in front of him, and for a moment he looks away from me, swallowing thickly.

Have I misjudged the situation?

Panicking, I word vomit, "I...you said...I just thought... it's stupid." I turn on my heel, determined to make a beeline to my bedroom again.

"Stop." Miller's voice is strained and commanding, halting me in my tracks, but I don't turn to face him.

Embarrassment settles on my chest, feeling like a hot iron's placed against it.

I jump when Miller's hand touches my shoulder, brushing my blonde hair away from my skin. Peeking behind at him, I meet his gaze, still equal parts nervous and turned on.

"How have we only known each other for a day, Snow Angel? This is crazy." His voice is low as he nuzzles his nose against the side of my cheek before pressing hot kisses against me.

Slowly, he works his way from my jawline, down my neck, to my shoulder, then turns me to face him. "The things you're doing to me in here." Placing my hand in his, he rests it on his chest over his heart, letting it linger for just a minute before he brings it down to rest over the impressively large bulge in his jeans. "And here... You're goddamn perfect," he growls.

With his free hand, his fingers find my chin and he grasps it, tilting my head back to kiss me in a deep, soul-altering kiss.

All I can do is whimper into his mouth as our tongues fall into a passionate exploration. He lets go of his hand that covers mine and allows it to wander across my body, sending shivers of need through me.

Walking us backward, his fingers find my bra and he unclasps it, the weight of my breasts forcing it to fall. It slides down my arms, and hastily I remove it, never breaking the kiss.

The backs of my knees hit the side of the bed and I stumble, but Miller's firm palm on my back stops me from falling. We kiss for a while longer before pulling apart.

Hooking his thumbs into the top of my panties, he pulls them down, sinking to his knees as he follows the garment down my legs. "Too much too soon?" he questions with a hint of hesitation in his tone.

I shake my head. "No. I want this. I want you."

Stepping out of my panties, I kick them to the side, so

all I'm left wearing is the red satin bow around my waist. Miller's eyes glitter with need as his touch floats up my legs, his hands stopping at my upper thighs.

When our gaze connects, an unexpected surge of power courses through me. This rugged, handsome man is on his knees right now, for me, on *Christmas*. Winding my fingers through his hair, I gently play with the silky strands.

Our eyes connect as he looks up at me, and my heart skips a beat. My core throbs, silently begging for his touch.

"Do you taste like Christmas, *Holly*? Like gingerbread, or maybe candy canes?"

"Are you going to find out?" I ask boldly, despite the slight shake in my hand lying awkwardly by my side.

"I don't think I've ever wanted anything more." Sliding his hands closer to the apex of my thighs, he uses his thumb to pull my lips apart and holds me steady with his other hand. My knees grow weak when he brushes over the most sensitive part of me, and I inhale a sharp breath.

"Is this okay?" His thumb continues to flick back and forth over me, and I feel my arousal slicken with each movement.

"Mmm hmm," I hum, tipping my head back as I claw at his shoulders.

Then I cry out.

Tracing patterns with his tongue, Miller devours me, fulfilling his promise of learning what I taste like. Wrapping his hands around the backs of my thighs, he keeps me still, holding me in place while he takes his time.

But time isn't on our side. It's been forever since I've been with a man, and I'm confident no man I've dated has ever been this skilled with his tongue. It hardly takes him two minutes of finding the perfect rhythm before I'm screaming his name as my knees buckle. My body melts against him and, as he stands, he scoops my limp body into his arms before immediately dropping me on the bed.

Pulling his shirt overhead, Miller tosses it to the side then kicks off the rest of his clothes. Through hooded eyes, I watch as his impressive erection juts out from between his legs, standing at attention like it's fully ready for my command.

Kissing his way up my legs and to my lower belly, his lips stop just beneath the bow. Goosebumps form under his touch as he plays with the ends of it, loosening it with small tugs. "Time to unwrap my present."

"I thought you already did that."

"Not all of it." With a final tug, the ribbon falls free, pooling on either side of my waist. He pulls it out from under me and bunches it in his grasp. "Do you trust me?"

"Yes." My answer comes naturally.

"Scoot up."

Doing what I'm told, I scooch back on my bedding until my back hits my pillows. Miller follows me, walking on his knees until he's hovering over my body. Taking my wrists, he holds them in one hand while wrapping the soft ribbon around them.

My heart rate accelerates as he ties a knot in the

ribbon, then begins to tie my wrists to the metal rung of the headboard.

"Ever been tied up, Snow Angel?" he asks with a smirk, testing the durability of the knot by pulling against it.

"No." I shake my head.

"Just tell me if you aren't into it, and I'll untie you immediately."

"Okay." My voice is quiet as I watch him lean off the bed and grab his jeans. He searches his pocket until he finds his wallet. Flipping it open, he pulls out a condom.

From the looks of it, that thing's been in there since condoms were invented. He knows it too, because his brows crease together as he looks down at the nearly destroyed wrapper in his hand.

His hair flops in front of his eyes as he looks at me. "This might not be good anymore... Dammit. I'm so sorry, Zee. I don't even know how long this has been in there."

"Don't get laid much?" I regret the words the second they're floating in the air between us.

Horrified, his eyes widen, and I try to diffuse the situation by laughing, but it comes out awkward and shrill.

"Oh, my God! That was supposed to come out as funny! I'm so sorry! Of course you get laid frequently, look at you, who wouldn't want to fu—"

He cuts me off when he slams his lips back to mine, tilting my head back as his palm wraps around my neck and he pushes his thumb against my jaw.

Pulling away just slightly, he leaves his forehead pressed to mine. "I don't jump from woman to woman, and I've had that in my wallet for *months*. So, no, Elizabeth, I don't get laid much, and that's by choice. I don't go sticking my dick in just anyone."

"Oh."

"And it looks like today I won't be sticking my dick in you, either." He groans slightly, pressing a chaste kiss to my lips before he rolls off me, laying his head on the same pillow.

My hands are still tied up above my head, but I easily turn my head to look at him. "No, please do."

"Can't." He tosses the busted condom onto my stomach. "You might be the perfect woman for me, but I'd prefer to not risk impregnating you within twenty-four hours of meeting. Call me old-fashioned."

"You're old-fashioned." I sigh, cracking a smile. "But fine. If you untie me, I'll at least return the favor."

"Nope."

"No, you won't untie me?" Instinctually, my wrists pull against the ribbon, testing the knot myself.

"No, you won't return the favor. I have a strict 'Elizabeth comes twice first' rule that I must follow." Pushing himself back to a seated position, he turns to untie the ribbon, attempting to loosen the knot as I try to think of a solid response to that, but honestly, he's surprised me.

Realizing he's at an uncomfortable angle, Miller gives me a lopsided smile as he crawls over my body, straddling my waist. Leaning forward, he works on the knot for a moment and successfully frees me. The moment I'm able to move, I use it to my advantage and slide further down the bed until he's over my chest.

Leaning more upright on my elbow, I grip his shaft and start to stroke him from root to tip, watching as a wave of pleasure coasts across his features. "You know what they say about rules, right, Miller?"

Licking my lips, I flick my gaze to his, relishing in the way he's looking down at me with a heated stare, like he's hanging on by a thread. Just before I guide his length into my mouth, I smile coyly and tell him matter-of-factly, "They're meant to be broken."

Miller

Chapter Sixteen

I'm convinced Heaven isn't where you go after your soul leaves your body, it's actually here, on Earth, in between the warmth of Zee's lips.

Taking me as far back as her throat allows, her head bobs up and down my shaft, licking and sucking it like it's a goddamn candy cane.

"*Fuck*, Zee," I moan, grabbing onto the top of her head as she hums appreciatively, sending vibrations through my veins.

Still straddling her chest, I grit my teeth and force myself not to drive forward like my body's begging me to. It'd be so easy to slide down her throat from this angle and damn if that's not exactly what I want to do, but I don't want to hurt her.

My dick twitches as her delicate hands reach around to grab my ass, and she uses it as a way to take me down further.

I'll never last more than two minutes if she keeps sucking me like this.

Reaching straight down, I grip her breast, tweaking her nipple between my finger and thumb to see if she likes it, and I'm rewarded with a low moan from her throat.

Her moans are the sexiest thing I've ever heard, and I want every single one of them to be mine.

I've gone and lost my mind over this woman.

Releasing her nipple, I decide to play her game. Rules are meant to be broken *and* bent.

Twisting my arm, I reach between her legs and stroke her perfect pussy, dividing her lips and playing with the arousal that drips from her, pulling her juices up to her greedy little clit that's begging for my attention.

I'll gladly give it all the attention it deserves.

As I play with her pussy, Zee whimpers and moans against my dick, intensifying her suction as I wind her up further.

My balls begin to tighten and the last thing I want to do is come before she does. *I wonder if she's into dirty talk...*

"You're so damn wet, Elizabeth. Your pussy's practically begging me to slide into you. Are you thinking about how good I'd feel filling you inch by inch?"

"Yes," she moans from around my shaft. Bringing her hand up to join her mouth, she wraps it around my base.

Pushing a finger into her, it slides in without resistance, the sound distinct and sexy as hell. I pump it in and out a few times before adding another, and use my thumb to strum her clit like it's my own personal guitar.

"I can't wait to slide into you, Zee. I just know your pussy will take me so well, just like your sexy little mouth is. Your lips look perfect around my dick, Snow Angel. I wish you could see."

She hums around my dick again, and her eyes start to water, dripping down the sides of her cheek. My fingers are soaked, and I can feel her walls clench around them. She's so responsive to my touch, so greedy in the best way possible.

Pulling off me suddenly, her fingertips dig into the tops of my thighs. "Miller, I'm coming. Yes. YES."

"Say my name again," I coax, thrusting my fingers into her as her hips lift off the bed.

"*Miller*," she pants through strangled breaths.

"Again."

"Miller." My name combines with a squeaky moan as her body drops to the bed like she'd been levitating.

But she doesn't miss a beat, and grabs my dick again and tugs it into her mouth. Groaning with pleasure, I look down at her as she pumps and sucks me, staring up at me. The sight is nearly too much to handle, and I recognize the signs of my release nearing.

Swirling my fingers inside her one last time, I bring them to my mouth and lick Zee's arousal from them. Her eyes widen as she watches, whimpering as I take my time.

The combination of her taste in my mouth and the feeling of her tongue on my shaft is my undoing, and I'm so damn close it's hard to hold it off any longer. "I'm about to come," I grunt, and there's a silent question in the air.

She answers it by sucking me harder, holding my dick and my leg tightly so I can't pull away. My release hits me with the force of a freight train. Weaving my fingers in her hair, I hold her head and roar as she swallows me down.

"Look at you, swallowing every last drop I had to give. You took me so well, so perfectly, Zee. How'd I get so lucky?" My fingers brush down the side of her cheek and to her chin as she releases me from her mouth and licks her lips. A small amount of my cum drips from her mouth, so I swipe at it with my thumb, pushing it back into her mouth.

She takes it eagerly, her eyes fluttering closed as my finger rests against her tongue. She swirls it around, and I hear her skin slap as she presses her thighs together.

Moving off her, I lay on my side, resting on my elbow. "That was—"

"Amazing," she finishes. Leaning down, I kiss her, tasting myself as our tongues meet.

As if she can't get enough, her hand finds my dick again, still half-mast, and she leisurely strokes it.

"You can't keep doing that unless you want me to take you bare, Elizabeth."

"Don't tempt me with a good time," she quips, and I fall back onto her pillow, groaning.

"That requires a conversation, *at least*, and right now, I think we're both in too much of a sex-induced fog for that."

Before she can answer, I roll and swing my legs off the bed so I can stand. Walking around to the side she's closest to, I scoop her up into my arms and walk her into her bathroom.

"What are you doing?" she asks as I place her on her feet in the middle of the small bathroom rug.

Pushing the shower curtain aside, I turn the faucet so it'll warm.

"You said a long shower was on your Christmas to-do list, so you're starting with that, Snow Angel."

"Are you joining me?" Her hand floats up to the center of chest, and she drums her fingers against my skin.

"Not a chance."

Zee's brows meet as she frowns.

The water feels hot against my hand when I test it again, so I turn to face her fully. Bringing my palm to her neck, I push against it gently until she's flat against the wall, then I kiss her. My fingers tease her entrance, and instinctually, her hips move against my touch. All I want to do is touch her, unable to get enough of her body now that I've had a small taste.

I can't wait for more.

The small bathroom starts to cloud with steam as I slip two fingers inside her, letting the heel of my hand rub against her clit. I pin her against the wall with my hand around her neck. "If I get into that shower, I'll end up inside of you." My tongue licks the seam of her mouth and she opens it eagerly, moaning as I find a pace that has her writhing against the wall from where she stands.

"I can't come again," she mewls, her eyes closing from

her body's overstimulation from pleasure. "Please—so sensitive, Miller."

"Shh. You can come again, and you will. You're already so close, Snow Angel. I can feel it. Your greedy little pussy is begging me for another orgasm. Has no one been taking care of it, beautiful? A pussy like this deserves to be worshiped. It needs to be *kissed* daily."

Her head shakes, but she doesn't answer me. Beneath my palm, I feel her swallow, her neck muscles constricting under my hold.

Bringing my head level with her ear, I whisper. "I'll worship it every goddamn day if you let me, Elizabeth. I'll worship *you*."

"Miller!" she screams again, her body practically falling as every ounce of energy is expelled into this orgasm. Her arms fly around my neck as I let go of hers so I can wrap my arm around her waist. I'm still fingering her pussy as it clenches around me, and walk us backward until I'm sitting on the side of the bathtub.

The hot spray of the shower meets my back, and I pull her to sit on my leg. Her legs spread to accommodate my fingers that refuse to leave her warmth, but they slow to a lazy stroke as I rub inside of her while she comes down fully from her orgasm.

Placing her hand on mine, she stops my motions, and I pull my hand from between her thighs. My fingers glisten as I drop my hand to my thigh, and she lays her head against my shoulder.

"I'm not sure I can stand in there." She lets out a small, breathy laugh. "You've literally made my knees weak."

"Do you want me to draw you a bath instead?"

"Mmm. That sounds amazing."

Kissing the side of her head, I lift her and place her to sit next to me, then turn to work on her bath. Along the bathroom counter is an arrangement of salts and bubble bath, so I fix it up to the best of my ability, making sure the shower curtain is completely out of the way, before I lift her legs and spin her on the ledge of the tub, dipping her feet into the water first.

She winces and lifts her legs out of the water a little.

"Too hot?"

"Just a smidge." She reaches and turns the water to cool slightly.

Looking around the steamy bathroom, I see a candy cane scented candle and a lighter on the opposite side of the sink, so I light it and set it on the ledge of the tub.

"What else can I get for you?

"Nothing, but you can join me."

Smirking, I shake my head. "It's cute that you think I'll fit in there."

"I won't be long, then."

Kissing the top of her head, I wink. "Take your time. I'll see if I can find us a movie to watch. Maybe I'll see if Potato feels like bonding yet."

"Don't get dressed." She bites her lip, her eyes dropping to my dick for a second.

"I *have* to," I stress. "Trust me, the rest of today will be torture trying to keep my hands off you. Now, time to relax."

With a final kiss on her head, I leave the bathroom in search of my clothes, her humongous cat, and my phone so I can look at the menus of nearby Chinese restaurants.

In that order.

"Okay, wait, tell me again what happened." Zee's laughing so hard, her fork bounces with every bout of laughter and a fried dumpling slides off it, landing on her plate with a small splat.

I shrug. "Lincoln thought he was tough shit and could handle the cold. I challenged him to spend five minutes outside on the porch, naked, to see if his balls could handle the shrinkage."

"And you stole his clothes."

"How was I supposed to know the most popular group of girls would walk down my road at that exact moment?"

"You didn't have to steal his clothes!" Tears stream down her face as she sets her fork down onto her plate, sliding it off her lap and onto the coffee table.

"I was *fourteen.*"

"You were a menace."

"At least he didn't know who they were! He only knew they were hot. It's not like he had to face them at school after break."

"True, but that was still mean."

"Says the woman who can't stop laughing."

"I never said it wasn't funny!"

Zee and I have spent the day lounging in each other's arms, watching the same romantic plot line over and over, just in different cities and states. At one point, we both fell asleep, and I swear I don't think I've slept that well in ages. We shared a mug of hot chocolate, ate one too many Christmas cookies, and Potato even did that thing cats do where they rub up against your leg a few times.

Zee says that's a good thing—I'm winning him over.

Today has been amazing, but the last movie, though, I felt a small shift in her. It was a movie she'd never seen before—one I can't remember the name of, they're all almost the same anyway—about a woman whose mother died, so she went back to her small town to clean out the house, and ended up falling for the neighbor.

She seemed to zone out after the mother's death was introduced into the storyline, which was within the first fifteen minutes.

I suggested we turn it off, but she didn't want to. Instead, she watched the full hour and thirty-seven minute movie with glassy eyes.

As much as I don't want to force Elizabeth to tell me about things she's not ready to talk about, despite all the laughter and fun we're having, there's a distance in her that wasn't there a couple of hours ago, and I fear right now she's a prisoner of her own thoughts.

When we've finished our dinner, I take the empty plate

from her lap and go make myself useful in the kitchen, feeling her eyes on me as I clean up. I ignore the pull to her and instead focus on putting away the leftovers, and washing the plates and utensils.

After wiping down the sink, I turn and find her with her head on her hands, her elbow leaning against the kitchen counter. With her hair piled on top of her head, and her face free of any stitch of makeup, she looks effortlessly beautiful.

Teasing, I ask, "See something you like?" and flip the towel over my shoulder.

"Actually, I do. I've never had a man do the dishes in my kitchen before. I think I might keep you."

"I hope you do." Walking over to her, I wrap my arms around her waist and pepper kisses against her cheek.

She sighs, melting into me.

"Are you okay?" I tread lightly.

"Yeah, why wouldn't I be?"

"You've just seemed a little distant since that last movie."

"Oh. It was just a little heavy."

"You can talk to me, you know. My aunt says I'm a pretty good listener."

"I trust Tina's opinion. It's just... I don't want to tell you, and have it change how you see me. Sometimes the grief hits me out of nowhere, and when it does, I see the way people look at me."

"With concern?"

"With pity."

"Zee—"

"Come on." She grabs my wrist. "This conversation requires the couch."

"I have a better idea." I lace my fingers through hers and pull her toward her bedroom, turning off light switches as we pass.

Leaving the light off, I carefully walk us to her bed and toss back her duvet. Stripping down to my boxers, I crawl under her covers, holding the blanket for her to follow.

She does and lies with her back to my chest. I curl my arms around her, pulling her close.

"It happened over the summer." She lets out a shuddering breath. "My parents, brother, and I went out to dinner on a Saturday night. It was a little later than we normally go to eat, but I had to work, so they waited until I got off. My brother picked up my parents on the way, and I met them there. We went to a small Italian restaurant, my parents' favorite place. Everything went perfect, our food came out quick, everything tasted delicious. There was laughter and happiness as we caught up with each other after having not seen each other for almost two weeks. That was unusual for my family—we typically saw each other at least once a week. It's always just been the four of us, and we were also close…"

Her voice cracks, and I pull her tighter to my body, kissing the back of her head.

"I told my parents I wanted to treat them since we were celebrating their anniversary, but my dad pulled that trick where he said he was going to the bathroom, and secretly paid the bill instead. When we were done, we said our goodbyes. My mom told me she would call me in the morning, and we left. I got on the road first... I'll never forget that I got on the road first. I should've waited until they left. *They* should've gone first. There were three of them, and one of me..."

She starts to shake in my arms, sobs racking through her body. Lacing our fingers together, I try to console her as best as I can. "Shh, Snow Angel, it's okay. You don't have to keep going. I'm here. I've got you."

"As they were turning onto the freeway entrance, a car coming the opposite direction didn't stop at the light. He didn't even slow down. He just kept going, and T-boned them. Their car spun out of control, Miller. It crashed into the guardrail, and they died on impact. My entire family— my world—*gone*."

Bile rises in my throat as Zee cries in my arms, the mental image of the accident playing over and over in my head. Anger starts to course through me, too. *Was the driver drunk? How had he not seen the red light? The car?*

"It should have been me," she cries, clutching onto my hand tightly as she buries her head into the pillow. "They should have left first."

"You can't think like that, Elizabeth," I bite, trying not to let my anger penetrate into my voice. But I'm so mad— this type of accident is preventable. *Just fucking pay atten-tion to the road.* "I know it hurts, baby, but there isn't anything *you* could have done to stop it."

She nods her head and twists in my arms, flipping over

to face me. Pressing her face against my chest, her tears soak my skin and I let her cry. I don't tell her it's okay, or try to change how she's feeling. Instead, I hold her tight and hope that it brings her some comfort.

Eventually, when she's calmed down, I press a soft kiss against her forehead. "Thank you for trusting me enough to share that."

"Please keep it between us. I don't like to talk about it." Her voice is quiet—drained. I wish this wasn't how we were ending our Christmas. My heart feels heavy...I can't imagine how hers feels.

"Of course, Snow Angel."

Snuggling tighter against me, she kisses my chest, and having her close starts to melt some of my negative thoughts away. "Merry Christmas, Miller. Thank you for making today less lonely."

A lump forms in my throat, and I nod, feeling the foreign sting of tears prickle my eyes. I think about the day, and her. How I met her just last night, as she came crashing into my life, taking some firs with her on the way.

What a whirlwind today has been. Unbelievable, in all the best ways.

Soft breaths of air puff against my skin, and I know Elizabeth is on the verge of falling asleep. Sleep threatens to take me too, but there's still so much heaviness in my heart as I hold her close, wishing I could take the pain she's feeling away from her and harbor it inside my body.

She shouldn't have to carry it all herself.

Closing my eyes, I swallow thickly as my brain spirals,

replaying everything she just told me as clips from the day flicker through my mind. I want to protect this woman from anything life throws at her, including her own grief. I want to only see her smile, and hear her laugh, because that's what she deserves in life—happiness.

Not this.

No one deserves this.

Only time will help heal her, though, and logically, I know there's nothing I can do to interfere with that process.

One thing's for certain, though, now that she has me, she'll never have to spend another holiday alone.

Chapter Seventeen

I wake up with a heaviness in my chest—a feeling like I can't breathe. Something startled me from my deep sleep, and as my eyes fly open, I quickly figure out the source of the panic.

Potato's vibrant blue eyes stare down at me with contempt, as he sits on top of me with a paw in the air, caught mid-assault.

Now I see what woke me.

"Must you always swat at me?" I grumble and pick him up off my chest using both hands, tossing him as gently as I can onto the bed next to me. With his size, he plops and gives me a disgruntled meow. Settling himself into a lying position, he stares at me expectantly.

Beside me, Miller stirs. His arms wrap around my body, and he ends up smacking Potato with the back of his hand. Angry, Potato jumps from the bed and runs to hide.

"I'm really striking out over here with him, aren't I?" Miller grumbles, pulling me closer.

"It could be worse, but yeah, it seems like every step you take forward you then knock yourself three steps back."

"Don't worry, I'll figure out how to get in his good graces."

"New goal?"

Nuzzling my neck, Miller starts to kiss his way up and pulls my earlobe into his mouth teasingly. "New life ambition. If you two are a package deal, I need to learn how to make him love me."

"Wow, already going for the L word, huh?" I feel my body start to ignite, but I can't let things progress despite really wanting to. According to my clock, I've overslept, which is very out of the norm for me and now I only have one hour before I'm due to leave. "Ugh. The last thing I wanna do is go to work today. Can't we just stay in bed?"

"As much as I want to say yes, I also need to be getting back to Julian. There's a lot to do at the tree farm today, and I didn't ask anyone to tend to my animals."

"They've been out all night?" A chill runs through me. *Those poor babies.* It's so cold up there, and no one was there to care for them, since I selfishly kept their owner all to myself.

"No, they weren't. It snowed so much overnight on Christmas Eve that I kept them in their houses yesterday. But that just means I'm going to have extra clean up to do today." He wrinkles his nose. "And the chickens are probably mad at me."

"Do they like to roam in the snow?" *That seems really cold for their feet.*

Miller brushes some of the hair away from my face, tucking it behind my ear. "No, they like attention. If I don't go out and talk to the girls at least twice a day, there's hell to pay."

My heart melts a little. *He's a good chicken dad.* "That's so cute. I can't wait to meet them."

"Well, what are you doing for New Year's Eve? Can you come up?" His eyes light up as he asks the question.

"I could probably arrange that. You don't have any fun plans already?"

"The only thing I have planned is dinner with my aunt and uncle. After that, I was planning to go home to find a video from last year's ball drop to watch, then turn in early."

I hesitate, looking across my bedroom at nothing in particular. The thought of seeing Miller's family again, after wholeheartedly leaning into the role of Holly North, Lincoln's girlfriend, is unnerving.

"How am I supposed to face Tina and Tim after lying to them? Do they still think I'm with Lincoln? Do they know you left on Christmas and came after me? What am I supposed to say to them—how do I explain myself?" The avalanche of words spill from my lips as my brain rapid-fires questions at me. My heart hammers in my chest, and

I feel like I need to pace the room. I try to pull out of Miller's arms, but he keeps me firmly in his hold.

I feel like this is a conversation I need to have with Lincoln, but Lincoln isn't in this room. Miller is.

So I start with him.

"When you followed me on Christmas, what did you say to them before you left?"

Sitting up in my bed, Miller shrugs. "Nothing really. I just gave my aunt a hug and told them I was sorry, but I had to go. I'm a grown man, Zee. I don't need to explain myself to my aunt and uncle."

My brows furrow together. "Don't you, though? You abruptly left their house on Christmas!"

"I usually don't stay long after breakfast and presents, anyway. I'm not really the type of guy who lingers. I keep busy. They know that."

"Do you think Lincoln said anything?"

"I highly doubt it, but I can call him and ask if it'll make you feel better."

"I just don't know how I'm going to explain myself."

"There's nothing to explain."

"Are you kidding me?" I toss my hands into the air. "There's *everything* to explain. I showed up at their house using a fake name, pretending to be their son's girlfriend!"

Miller nods, squeezing my hand. "I guess you're right. We'll just have to start with your name, then. Introduce you as who you really are, tell them you were hesitant to use your real name with strangers. I don't really care if my aunt and uncle think I stole you from Lincoln—we don't have to explain that side of the story if you don't want to."

"I don't think it's about what I want, Miller. We need to do what Lincoln wants, since he's the one who was worried about maintaining a certain image in front of his parents."

Rubbing his thumb against his lips, he stares at the wall, and is quiet for a second. I long to know what he's thinking about, but I don't ask. After a couple minutes, he nods. "Whatever you want to do, Zee. If you want to call Lincoln and get on the same page, then let's get him on speakerphone. If you don't want to tell my aunt and uncle *anything* right now, then I'll cancel dinner with them and make you dinner at my cabin instead."

"Don't cancel dinner with them," I blurt, shaking my head. "I feel like I ran out so abruptly, and they were so kind to me." Looking at the bed, I lower my voice to just above a whisper, my heart aching. "It felt like I had a family again."

Miller squeezes my hand again, then uses his finger to lift my chin. "You do."

"That's sweet. You all hardly know me, though."

"You have a knack for making people feel like they've known you forever." He leans over and gives me a soft kiss on the lips. "And trust me, I know my family. I'm not the only one not willing to let you go."

Cupping my cheek, he rubs his thumb across it softly. "What time did you say you have to go to work?"

"I need to be there in less than an hour, and I like to

leave at least 20 minutes early. Sometimes the drive is quick and other times there's traffic."

"Then you better get up. Go get dressed, and I'll make you a cup of coffee. Do you eat breakfast? I can scramble some eggs?"

"I prefer to drink my calories in the morning. Thank you though. If you're hungry, help yourself to whatever you want."

"I'm good. I usually just start with a cup of coffee too."

"Okay," I tell him as I crawl over his lap. Straddling him, I take his head in between both of my palms, and kiss him tenderly.

I could stay in bed and kiss him all day.

When things start to get heated, I force myself to pull away, knowing if I don't, I'll end up being late for work. "Okay, I really need to get up now."

Forcing myself off his lap, I go straight to the bathroom, and run the faucet so the water will warm, before realizing the entire reason I was startled awake this morning.

Potato never got his breakfast.

Turning off the stream of water, I pad down the hallway to my kitchen, and stop dead in my tracks when I see Miller popping the lid off of a can of wet food, with a spoon already in hand. Rubbing against Miller's legs, Potato meows excitedly as Miller scoops the food into his bowl.

As stupid as it is, my eyes well up with tears at the

sight, and I slowly back away to return to getting ready for work.

Miller's so effortlessly considerate, and even though it feels too good to be true, I know it's not. I spent enough time with the Stokes family to know the kindness in their hearts, and I feel I have a pretty good read on Miller's personality.

He's a good man, and good men like him are hard to find.

"Hey boss, how was your holiday?" Genesis asks from behind the counter as I walk toward her, having just dropped my stuff in the break room. The bookstore is quiet today, with only a few patrons looking around, presumably shopping for something new to spend their gift cards on.

"It was actually really good. How was yours?"

"Loud, chaotic, and so much fun." She grins brightly. "My family is crazy, in the best way. You should've taken me up on the offer to come over. I laughed so hard, I almost peed at one point during a game of Cards Against Humanity."

"That sounds like fun! Maybe next time you guys have a big gathering."

And I meant it this time. I'm slowly beginning to realize that I need to put myself out there again—spend time with people. I've missed it, and I hadn't realized how much until all of my crazy holidates.

"What did you end up doing?"

Part of me hesitates, wondering how much personal information I should divulge to a coworker—my employee. But Genesis is also a friend, and I value that side of our relationship more than maintaining professionalism.

Not to mention, she's the one who gave me the idea to become Holly North, sort of.

Relenting, I spill every last detail, minus the private details between me and Miller. I admitted that her words played on repeat in my head until I finally had the insane idea to re-download the SparksFly app and edit my profile, then I told her about each of the dates, ending, of course, with how I spent my Christmas.

She listens intently, eyes widening with certain details, and as soon as I finish recounting everything and take a deep breath, she squeaks loudly with excitement. Clapping her hands together, she squeals, "Girl, you realize your entire month of December has been like something right out of a Christmas movie, right? Like, someone get Hollywood on the phone, ASAP. Why didn't you tell me any of this as it was happening?"

I clench my teeth together in a purposely awkward smile and laugh. "Honestly, I felt a little weird. I *am* your boss."

"Okay, yeah, but you're also my friend. I can't believe you held out on me."

Leaning against the counter, she props her head up on her fist. "So you ditched the doctor to be with the lumberjack?"

"I was never actually with the doctor. And I don't think Miller's a lumberjack, Gen."

"He owns a tree farm?" she questions.

"Well, yes."

"Therefore, he owns an ax?"

"Probably..."

"Lumberjack," she concludes.

I start giggling, thinking about the words I used in my head a couple of days ago. "More like a lumber *snack*."

Genesis howls in laughter. "Oh my God, new favorite phrase. Why is that not trending on socials?"

"I don't know, but it should be."

"Send me a picture of him?"

"No! I just met him. How am I supposed to have a picture of him?"

"Please, from the sounds of it, you two are already in a committed relationship, practically planning your wedding."

Covering my face with my hands, I shake my head. "You're crazy! No, we're not."

"From everything you just told me, that man is in love. L.O.V.E."

"It's been a day! Literally! We met on Christmas Eve."

She rolls her eyes at me, crossing her arms. I follow her stance, and look out at the sales floor. "It doesn't matter," Genesis continues. "When you know, you know, and no amount of time makes a difference. Do you like him?"

"Yes, of course."

"But I bet when I just asked you that, you thought 'like doesn't feel strong enough'."

"How did you—"

"Because you have that look."

"What look? You need to stop reading all the romance books in the store, Gen. I have no look."

"You do. Just trust me on this. You may not see it right now, but give that man another date, and you'll be feeling it."

"What if he's not?" I ask, biting the side of my thumb. I glance over at her, and she rolls her eyes at me again.

"There is no way that man is not already head over heels."

"I think you exaggerate."

"And I think you don't give yourself enough credit. You deserve happiness, Zee. Embrace it. This is your Christmas wish. Even if you didn't realize you were wishing for it, Santa delivered. Now, how many letters do I need to write before Santa will deliver *me* a lumber snack? Did you post-mark to somewhere specific? Add it to your Amazon cart?"

We both start laughing, and I feel so lighthearted and carefree. I'm glad I told her everything. Her excitement has only amplified mine, making me excited about this new thing with Miller.

I want to call him. I want to see him again.

Knowing that I have to wait six days feels like too long. It feels unreasonable. Pulling out my phone, I send him a text.

> Do you think we could figure out a time to see each other before New Year's Eve?

> It's like you took the words right out of my mouth. Now that I'm not with you, six days feels excruciating. When is your next day off?

> I won't have another day off until Sunday.

> Are you already off on New Year's Eve?

> Yes, and New Year's Day.

> I can come back on Sunday.

> Can I take you on a proper date?

> I'd love that.

> Then it's settled. I'll see you Sunday.

> I can't wait. Got to go, I'll talk to you later?

> I'll call you tonight.

Genesis is staring at me as I push my phone back into my pocket, waiting with bated breath for me to update her on what was just said. Rolling my eyes, I walk away and pretend to organize the back counter.

"So?" She follows me over to it. "I know you're not

going to pretend like you didn't just talk to him. What did he say? What did you say? Fill me in."

"You're nosy!"

"You brought me into this! Now it's your duty to update me."

Picking up a stack of books, I shrug. "You saw how quick the text conversation was. He's coming over Sunday. Wants to take me on a real date."

She squeals in delight. "What are you guys going to do?"

"We haven't discussed it. Any suggestions?"

Gen purses her lips. "You could go to the zoo. Go see the giant pandas. They're so cute!"

"My membership expired," I counter. "What else?"

"Hmm. You could have him take you to the theater in Liberty Station, go watch a movie in the reclining chairs and have a drink."

"That sounds fun. I wonder if there's anything good playing right now. I could look."

"Oh!" she blurts. "I know! Go to Coronado and go ice-skating at the hotel. I'm pretty sure they're still doing s'mores on the beach through the New Year. That could be romantic!"

I lean against the counter, grinning. "That sounds like a lot of fun, actually."

"You should do it! Sip on some hot cocoa, skate around. Then get cozy by the fire, if ya know what I mean." She knocks her elbow into my rib cage, waggling her brows.

"Why do you always have such good ideas?"

She shrugs. "It's why you pay me big bucks. Hey, by the way, is that hot doctor you dumped single now, or what?" Her smile is devious as she tosses a wink over her shoulder, then turns into business mode and addresses the customer who's approaching the cash wrap. "Hi! Did you find everything you were looking for today?"

With a grateful heart, I shake my head as I laugh and walk onto the sales floor with books to put back, trying to ignore the urge to pull the phone out of my back pocket and start researching information for mine and Miller's first date.

Miller

Chapter Eighteen

I've made it through one full day of not seeing Zee, and I feel like I deserve a medal for that. I've spent every waking moment thinking of her, and when I close my eyes it's her I see in my dreams.

Being away from her feels like I've left something behind in San Diego, and I know it's my heart. It's in the palm of her goddamn hand, and I never want her to give it back.

I thought falling in love overnight only happened in the movies, but she's proven me wrong. Elizabeth Ashford is all-consuming. A gale-force wind that blew into my life and inserted her presence, whether she meant to or not.

When my animals are tucked safely into their homes for the night, I head back into my cabin to grab the bag I packed earlier. I couldn't stand the thought of not seeing Zee tonight, so I made arrangements for my animals. Thankfully, a buddy of mine agreed to take care of them tomorrow and Sunday morning. It was a big ask, but I pay him well, and bribed him with promises of football, beer, and steak at my place next time his team plays. As soon as the plan was set in motion, I got ready to return to San Diego.

Slamming the door to the truck, I glance down at the clock as the engine warms up, and send Zee a quick text before I hit the road. She has no idea I'm on my way to surprise her, and I plan to keep it like that for as long as possible.

Thinking about you.

She's off in about thirty minutes, so I don't expect a response right away. Tossing my phone into the cup holder, I put on the radio and relax into my seat as I hit the road.

You'd never know it's the week between Christmas and New Year's by the way the tourists still flock to my small town, meandering around the different shops and eating their body weight in pie. The parking lots and streets are filled with vehicles, making the road out of town a little harder to navigate.

I've always hated this week—that awkward limbo between the two major holidays. It feels like time doesn't exist, and everything is just...*off*.

Or maybe I'm projecting what I've been feeling since I've been away from Zee.

The drive is smooth, the radio deejay keeping my

company through the winding back roads and bout of traffic as I drive through the town of Ramona.

When I make it to the outskirts of East County, I pick up my phone again and find a message waiting for me.

> Just walked through the door! So glad to be home. Potato was sitting in the middle of my kitchen table looking like he was plotting my murder.

Why?

> His bowl was empty.

I laugh and shake my head, keeping one hand on the wheel.

He's an eating machine.

I shouldn't be texting while I'm driving, but I can't help myself. Knowing that I'm so close to seeing her but still have a bit of a drive is the worst.

> He really is. How was your day?

It would have been better if you were here, but it was fine. Tended to the animals. Worked on cleaning up the tree farm.

> Did Tamar help?

I groan, knowing she's joking, but still feeling mildly

guilty. I opened up to her about mine and Tamar's past, which didn't paint me in the best light. In my defense, the more I told her, the worse it sounded. *And* I didn't think I'd see her again.

Ha. Ha.

The conversation goes silent, and I imagine her making herself some dinner, or fawning over Potato. After a while, I send her another text. There's only about ten minutes of drive time left, so I want to see what she's up to before I show up at her house unannounced.

What are you doing right now?

Soaking in the tub. My dogs are barking.

My dick stirs at the thought of her naked body slick with water.

Show me.

No way! I'm not a nude photo kinda gal.

I didn't say you had to be nude.

The messages halt for a moment and I wonder if I pushed her too much, until my phone vibrates in my hand. I practically drop it as I swipe the message quickly to open it.

"Goddamn," I breathe as a photo of Zee in the bath illuminates my phone. Bubbles are strategically placed over her breasts and lower body, but my imagination shows me everything I need to see. Her golden hair's piled on top of her head, and I can just make out the tops of her lashes and the tip of her nose as she angles the phone downward.

She's absolutely stunning.

My dick hardens as my thoughts run away with me and I think about all the filthy things I want to do to her.

God, you're so damn sexy.

I want you so bad right now.

I wish you were here...

Would I be in the bath with you if I was?

Yeah. We'd make it work. I could sit on your lap.

I could think of a lot of things you could do on my lap, Snow Angel.

Do you want to hear about them?

Yes.

I'll tell you if you lay back and touch yourself as I tell you.

I'd rather have you down my throat.

My eyes widen as the message comes through, and I have to reach down and adjust myself. Maybe this is a bad idea—God, why the hell do I keep hitting every goddamn light in this city?

Oh, really, Snow Angel? Do you want my cum in that pretty little mouth again?

Yes.

Fuck.

Are you touching yourself right now, Zee?

Yes.

Tell me how wet you are for me.

So freaking wet. My toy just slid in so easily.

You brought your toy with you? Wishing it was me?

I'd rather it be you. I've thought about you nonstop. I touched myself to the thought of you last night and came with your name on my lips.

Fuck, you're driving me crazy.

Tell me what you'd do if you had me on your lap.

I'd start by gripping your hips and grinding you on top of me. I'd slide you up and down my shaft, coating it in your juices.

Play with your clit, Snow Angel. I want
your pussy to throb as much as my dick
is right now.

I am. I'm imagining it's you who's
touching me. Your fingers, not mine.

Damn straight. It's me touching you
right now.

And in a couple of minutes, I really will be.

As soon as the stoplight I'm sitting at turns green, I peel away, my tires skidding against the pavement when I step on the gas. I'm about to turn into Zee's apartment complex, when another text comes through from her.

It's another photo, and this time it's of her lower body, the bubbles placed so it doesn't show much, but I can clearly see her hand disappearing under the water and between her legs.

I take the first parking spot I can find and rip the keys from the ignition, practically running into her building. Jamming my finger into the elevator's call button, I tap my foot impatiently as my fingers fly over my phone's touch-screen keyboard.

You're so sexy. If I was there, I'd rip you
from that bathtub and you'd be sitting on
my face, dripping wet as you ride it.

I'm close, Miller.

The elevator pings, and I rush inside, slamming my

finger against the button for her floor's level, then again on the button to close the doors.

> Don't you dare come yet.

> Are you touching yourself while you think about me?

Staring up at the numbers as they ascend, I mutter under my breath. "C'mon, stupid elevator, go faster."

> I'd rather be touching you.

When the doors open, I fly out of them and am in front of Zee's door in a flash, rapping my knuckles across the white-painted wood.

My heart gallops inside my chest as I wait to hear her footsteps approach the door. With my head practically pressed against it, I listen, hearing nothing inside of her apartment as I wait.

Every fiber of my being itches to break the door down to get in there with her, but I keep waiting, trying to urge myself to calm down. I'm so wound up, I feel like I might spontaneously combust on her doorstep if I don't have her in my arms soon.

In my hand, my phone vibrates, alerting me of another incoming message.

> So come touch me then.

Practically snapping my phone from how tightly I squeeze it as I read her message, I shove it into my pocket and rap my knuckles against the door again, much louder this time.

My forehead knocks into the wood as I groan with frustration, still not hearing any signs of movement in her apartment after a few moments.

Slapping my open palm against the door, I growl, "Open the door, Elizabeth."

This time, my heart flip-flops when I hear the sound of her footsteps.

"Miller?" she questions through the wood as the sound of the deadbolt disengages.

My chest rises and falls, my voice gruff as I confirm, "It's me."

Her front door flies open, and the second my eyes fall on her, she takes my breath away. Her hair is messy, tied up on top of her head, and all she's wearing is a sage green bath towel that she holds against her breasts. Her skin is slick from the bathtub, bubbles still clinging to her skin as water droplets slide down her legs.

I can't even string together a sentence as I walk through her door, slamming it behind me, and reach for her towel. Pulling it from her body, it falls to her feet. My arms encircle her and I slam my lips against hers, kissing her deeply as I walk her backward through her apartment.

"How are you here?" she asks between kisses.

My hand drifts down, cupping between her legs so I can feel her. "Drove."

She's soaked, and not from her bath. She was touching herself, and fuck if that doesn't make me even harder just thinking about it. "Did you get yourself off, Snow Angel?"

She hisses through her teeth as I use two fingers to play with her entrance. "Obviously you drove." Her calves hit her unmade bed and I lower her down on her sheets. She moans, then shakes her head. "No, but I was close."

"I can tell." Kissing my way down her body, I swipe my tongue up her seam, tasting her like I've been thinking about doing for the entire duration of my drive.

It takes every ounce of restraint I can muster to pull myself back to standing. Tugging my shirt overhead, I reach into my pocket and pull out a condom from the pack I bought yesterday, before stripping free of my pants and boxers.

"I've driven myself insane today thinking about you. Do you have any idea how hard it's been to not be here? You've consumed every thought I've had since I left on Thursday. I missed you."

"I missed you too." Zee lifts to her elbows and watches as I roll the condom on my shaft.

Pressing my knee into her mattress, I crawl over her body and catch her lips with mine. My muscles strain under my body weight as I hold myself above her. She slides her hands up my forearms until her hands tangle in the hair that rests on the nape of my neck.

Lowering myself onto her, her legs spread on instinct, widening to accommodate my body with hers.

"You've enchanted me, Zee. I've never felt this way about anyone."

Holding my shaft in my hand, I rub it up and down her entrance, teasing her before I push in just slightly. We moan in unison as she stretches around me. Slowly, I ease in further, stopping for a few seconds with every bit I press, so she has the chance to adjust.

When she's taken me fully, I rest my forehead against hers and marvel at the gift I've been given this year. She's everything I didn't know I wanted or needed.

As if she can read my thoughts, she whispers, "Don't let me go," and wraps her arms around my neck.

Sliding her foot against the back of my leg, I catch the bend in her knee with my arm, holding her leg as I adjust our position slightly.

"I have no intention of ever letting you go, Elizabeth," I say against her lips. And I mean it. *I'm going to marry this woman someday.*

Feeling her body relax with the promise of my words, I deepen the kiss, and our bodies begin to move as one.

Slow and controlled, I thrust into her, worshiping her body with mine. A million emotions roll through me all at once, strong and intense. I've never felt this way about anyone in the past, like I just admitted to her, but what I won't say is that connecting with her on this level stirs something with me that has laid dormant for my entire life.

She moans into my mouth as I kiss her, soft mewls

humming through me while I appreciate every curve of her body. My hand slides up her side, exploring, as my hips roll into her.

Her body feels like home.

"You feel so good, Miller," she whimpers, and the restraint I'm holding inside starts to sever. Picking up my speed, I press into her deeper and roll her clit between my finger and my thumb.

"How good, Snow Angel?"

"Oh, my God."

Licking her neck, I pull nearly all the way out of her, then slam back in. I'm rewarded with a heady moan, so I do it again, and then again, enjoying the sounds it draws from her.

"Your sexy little moans are enough to make me come right now, but *fuck*, I could stay in your pussy forever. It was made for me, Zee. You take me so well."

"You were made for me," she repeats, her voice breathy and strained.

"Fuck yeah, I was. How have I gone this long without you? Never again. You're mine, Elizabeth. You. Your body. Mine," *thrust*, "mine," *thrust*, "mine."

Sliding my arm under her, I lift her and lean back on my heels so she's straddling me in a seated position, and she shifts to ride me instead. From this position, I'm able to tangle my hand in her hair and kiss her. Her arms wrap around my neck as she bounces on my dick, taking me at different paces until she finds what works for her.

There's no telling where I end and she begins, and when her body begins to tense around me, I know she's close.

Snaking my hand between her legs, I brush my fingers against her clit to help her over the edge, and it takes seconds before she's crying out in pleasure, and I catch every moan in my mouth as I deepen our kiss. My grunts merge with her satisfied whimpers as my release slams into me with fury.

I come harder than I ever have, losing all control as my body responds to this unbelievable woman in my arms.

"Holy crap," she breathes, when we both finally catch our breath. I'm still inside her, sitting in the same position, neither of us wanting to break the contact.

Telling her I love her is on the tip of my tongue, but fear holds me back.

What if she doesn't feel the same? What if I ruin everything by telling her too soon?

Dropping my forehead to hers, I keep my thoughts to myself, and instead, hold her tight and hope that my body conveys what my mind forces me to keep to myself.

"Thank you," she whispers, surprising me when she pulls me from my thoughts.

"For what?"

"For taking away some of the loneliness."

My heart squeezes in my chest, not ready for the words that tumble from her lips because they're so bittersweet knowing her history. I want to take her pain away—hold her close and never let anything hurt her again.

Tell her you love her.

But I can't. Not yet.

Instead, I press my lips against her forehead and tell her, "You'll never be lonely again, Zee. I promise."

Zee

Chapter Nineteen

"Are you sure I can't help you clean up?"

Miller kisses me on the side of the head as he comes around to my side of the table. "No, you go get ready. Leave the kitchen to me."

Grinning, I nod my head. "You're too good to me."

Yesterday as we laid in bed after he surprised me by showing up at my apartment, I told him my idea to go ice skating and do s'mores on the beach for our date. I thought I'd be met with at least a little resistance, but Miller was all in for it.

Opting to not fight the crowds, we made dinner together in my small kitchen instead. The scent of roasted sweet potato, rosemary chicken, and asparagus still lingers in the air.

"It's just cleanup, Zee. Don't give me too much credit." Miller stacks our plates and carries them over to the trash can, scraping the remnants of food into it, before placing the dishes down gently in the sink.

While he waits for the water to warm, he adds soap to the sponge and rests his forearms on the edge as he looks over his shoulder at me. "Go."

"So bossy! Fine. I'll be ready in less than twenty."

"Take your time."

Heading into my bedroom, I find Potato lying on top of my pillow, and I sit down on the edge of the bed to give him some attention.

"What're your thoughts on all of this, big guy?" I scratch behind his ears, knowing I won't get a response. "I think he's a good one. A keeper."

Potato gives me a blank expression.

"I don't feel so lonely when I'm with him," I continue, as though the tubby feline understands exactly what I'm saying. "I know what you're thinking—it's all so fast. Part of me is waiting for the other shoe to drop, but I am optimistic that it won't. I have to be, Potato. There hasn't been much hope in my life lately, but Miller makes me think a little differently. I feel like I can see the good again."

A deep ache resonates in my chest and I picture the faces of my mom, dad, and brother. They would have loved Miller. My dad especially. But I know Miles would have been skeptical about how fast my new relationship has been moving. He was always protective of me.

A sob strangles in my throat, and before I know it's happening, tears stream down my face.

Potato looks at me with a bored expression, curling further into himself to take a nap. I should go get ready, but instead, I sit here, chest heavy, as I stare out my bedroom window with my hand perched on my cat.

I wish I had a time machine so I could go back to that day and just draw out our goodbyes a little longer. If we had just spent a little more time at that restaurant, maybe things would be different.

Maybe they wouldn't have been hit by that car.

Time seems to stand still, and I'm not sure how long I sit on the edge of my bed, but I'm pulled from my thoughts when I hear the water in the kitchen shut off. Realizing I need to get ready, I go into the bathroom and pull out my hairbrush, curling iron, and my makeup bag.

Being relatively low maintenance has its perks, and I'm finished in less than 15 minutes. When I come out of the bathroom, Miller is on the couch with a deep scowl on his face, staring down at his phone.

"What's wrong?" Sinking onto the cushion next to him, I place my hand on his thigh.

He pushes the side button, darkening his screen. "I was just texting with Lincoln. He's going to be at my aunt and uncle's on New Year's Eve."

"Is that a problem?" Sure, I may have fake dated Lincoln for a day, but it's not like we actually had feelings for each other—which Miller obviously knows.

"Not really, but he does want to tell my aunt and uncle the truth. He said the guilt is weighing on him. I told you we wouldn't have to tell them anything you weren't comfortable with, and now Lincoln is trying to derail that."

"Oh, well, you and I had already discussed it. I think it's what's best. I don't want there to be lies between us. They were so kind and welcoming, and I've already broken their trust."

His intentions are good. I know they are.

"I just don't want to put any more on you..."

Taking his hand in mine, I squeeze it. "It'll be fine, and if it's not, then we will figure it out then."

Miller wraps his arm around me and pulls me close. "You're right. Let's not dwell on it now. It's time for me to show off my ice-skating skills."

"Are you good at skating?"

"The best. I used to be pro." His smile is coy, like he's suppressing a laugh, and my eyes widen.

"Seriously?"

"No," he says through laughter. "I'm actually really terrible at ice-skating, so this should be interesting."

"Oh, no! That's not good."

"Why?"

"Because one of us needs to be good at it to carry the other."

"You suck at skating too?"

"Big time."

"Great. Well, at least we'll be embarrassed together."

The ice rink glitters from the Christmas lights around it, reflecting off the ice. Holiday music plays through the speaker system, still giving Christmas cheer even though it's about to be New Year's Eve.

Happiness oozes from every direction as families and couples skate. Tables are full of families enjoying hot chocolate together, and couples in cozy winter jackets and beanies line the bar. It's far busier than I thought it would be, but as we put our skates on, excitement tingles me, zipping around my bloodstream in a rush of endorphins.

"Are you ready for this?" Miller asks, taking my hand.

"Ready as I'll ever be. Hopefully neither of us ends up in the hospital."

"Don't worry, we know a good doctor if we need one."

I'm still laughing when Miller pulls me out onto the ice, and we clutch onto each other—and the wall—like fawns who are learning to walk. The ice is crowded with people of all skill levels, some gliding across it gracefully, and others not so much.

My legs tremble like a leaf as I try to get my bearings, but once I start grasping the concept better, I gain the confidence to let go of the wall.

You'd think I'd be better at this considering I love to rollerblade on the Mission Beach Boardwalk, but wheels on the bottom of a shoe feel much different than a blade.

What little confidence I have at the moment doesn't extend past me, though, because Miller looks like he might be ready to throw in the towel. Even holding onto the wall, he hunches over as he tries to be steady on his feet.

"How the hell do hockey players make this look so easy?" he grumbles as his legs start going in opposite directions.

"Well, I'm no figure skater, but if you stop thinking about it and just try to walk and glide, your body fills in the gaps."

Straightening himself, he lifts one arm out to the side while the other death grips the wall, and tries to do as I instruct, but ends up marching on the ice, which only makes me laugh harder.

After a couple minutes, he seems to get the hang of it.

At least for twelve seconds.

Growing cocky, he reaches for my hand, but it becomes his undoing. Completely losing his balance, he topples over, taking me down with him as he falls. Two sets of arms and legs go flying, and we both land on our butts on the cold, hard ice, laughing so much, we both struggle to breathe.

"I was doing so well!" I squeal, my cheeks sore from the wide grin on my face. "Why'd you have to pull me with you?"

"Me?" He gives me a sarcastic look of disbelief and shakes his head as he lays it on thick. "This was all you! I totally had it."

"Sure you did."

Sitting on the ice proves dangerous as skaters race past us, their blades getting far too close for comfort, and when a small child passes by paying no attention to us, I try to stand, which is much harder than it looks without grabbing onto something.

Falling again, Miller roars a laugh. "Let me show you how it's done." Reaching for the wall, he uses one hand to pull himself to a crouch, but ends up losing his balance *again* and topples back over.

Cursing under his breath, he repeats the process, and this time stands successfully, extending his hand for me. Surprisingly, he's able to pull me to my feet, and we end up clutching onto the side of the wall like it's our lifeline.

"Maybe ice-skating isn't for us," he admits. "I don't think either of us have the grace this sport requires."

"Are you saying I'm not graceful?"

"That's exactly what I'm saying." He tucks a piece of my hair behind my ear that's escaped from my beanie.

"Wow, tell me how you really feel."

"You know what I bet we both are good at?"

"What?"

"Devouring some s'mores." Miller looks longingly in the direction of the beach, then back at me with puppy dog eyes.

"We haven't even been skating for ten minutes!" I laugh, knowing he paid a lot of money for us to do this.

Miller shrugs, obviously not caring. "Personally, I think that's five minutes too long. But if you're still into it, we can struggle around the edge together."

"We at least should take a full lap! Come on, we can do this."

And we did, but it took us a full twenty minutes, and almost two more rounds of falling before we made it back to the entrance.

"I'm so sorry, sir, but our cabanas require a reservation in advance and unfortunately, they're all spoken for this evening." The hotel worker apologizes with a remorseful look on his face.

Miller glances at me. "I'm so sorry, I didn't know, otherwise I would've scheduled ahead."

"You shouldn't be the one apologizing. I suggested this date! I didn't know either."

Turning back to the worker, he asks, "There've been no cancellations? There isn't a waiting list?"

The man ponders Miller's question and looks down at his schedule book in front of him. "Give me just a second."

As the man scurries away, Miller turns to me. "We could always go to the hotel's gift shop, get some snacks, and pick a spot to hang out on the beach. Not quite the same, but if all else fails."

"That sounds perfect." I lean against him with my head on his chest. His arm circles around my waist. "Don't worry, we could also just go back to my place and hang out. It doesn't have to be fancy. I just want to spend time with you."

"I'm not going anywhere," he promises, kissing the top of my beanie-covered head.

The hotel worker comes back to his podium and looks around before dropping his voice. "I just got approval from my manager to open up one of the reserved cabanas. You have an hour before the party comes."

"That's all we need." Miller pulls his wallet from his pocket and hands the man a credit card. "Thank you."

"You'll be in cabana number eight." The worker pulls a box of graham crackers, two chocolate bars, and a bag of marshmallows from below his stand. "Roasting sticks are already in there, and a member of the waitstaff will be there to take your drink orders shortly. There is also a menu if you'd like anything else."

"Great, thanks." Gathering everything, Miller shifts the sweet treats into one arm so he can hold my hand with the other. I offer to take something, but he tells me he's got it.

My heart swells from how kind this man is. *No one's ever treated me like such a princess.*

As we walk along the beach, our steps are slow, heavy from the weight of our shoes against the sand. When we enter our cabana, it takes my breath away. Three of the four sides are enclosed so it's semi-private, and Christmas lights line the edges of the inside, brightly lit with multi-color bulbs. The small gas fire pit is already lit with a small fire burning, and there's plush seating arranged around it, overlooking the ocean. I bet the view is gorgeous during a clear summer day, and I make a mental note that we should come back for a staycation. Looking around, I locate the menu and the marshmallow skewers we were told would be here.

"This is so cute!" I tell Miller as I drop my purse on the couch, feeling giddy. He places the s'mores supplies down next to my purse, then turns to me with a serious expression on his face.

My heart drops, a flicker of ice instantly shooting through my veins. Taking both of my hands in his, he pulls us down to sit, then kisses my knuckles.

"Elizabeth, you know these last few days have been a dream. I've spent years up in my secluded little cabin, spending time with family, and working on my farm. Life's been good—comfortable—and I never felt like anything was missing. But then you tripped into my world, and suddenly, everything changed. I never realized my life was the equivalent of white Christmas lights until you came in and rehung them in multicolor hues. Everything's more vibrant and beautiful with you around, and I don't want to go back to how things were."

He looks down at our hands, still clasped together, and sighs deeply. "This is going to sound absolutely insane. Never for one second did I think I would *ever* be the guy to say this, let alone have this happen to him..."

He hesitates, and I wait with bated breath, not wanting to interrupt him. My heart is hammering in my chest as I wait, nerves coursing through me.

"But I'm trying to say... What I'm trying to say...is... I fell in love with you, Elizabeth. I love you."

My jaw slackens, completely stunned by his admission.

All at once, my brain and my heart go to war with each other, one screaming *it's too soon* while the other swells with happiness.

"You... You love me?"

"More than I ever thought possible," he says in earnest. "And I know it's fast—I'm not expecting you to feel the same. I just needed to tell you. It has been weighing heavily on my mind, and I needed to get it off my chest."

"No." Quickly, I let go of his hands and take his face between my palms, pressing my lips to his. "I love you too," I breathe, and kiss him again.

"Yeah?"

"Yes." The confirmation is barely audible before he slams his lips to mine again. Immediately, I wrap my arms around his neck and a small whimper leaves my chest.

As our kiss intensifies, his hands slide beneath the hem of my shirt, and he traces my spine as he pulls me closer. "I want you so bad. I can't keep my hands off you. It's like I have no self-restraint when you're in my vicinity."

The sound of laughter from a neighboring cabana rings into the crisp night sky, forcing me to pull away. Breathless and flustered, I turn to the box of graham crackers and give it a small shake. "Let's have some s'mores, then I'll let you take me home."

I hand him one of the skewers and he nods, then drifts his hand down to the bulge in his pants and shamelessly adjusts himself. "You're right—we need to keep it PG here. But how long did the guy give us? An hour? After that, you're mine, Elizabeth, and I don't care if I have to have you in the back of the car. I *will* have you."

His filthy promise ricochets into the deepest parts of my core, and I swallow thickly. "Sounds fair."

Picking up a marshmallow, Miller smirks as he stabs it onto the stick. "I have a very important question to ask you."

"Okay."

"Are you a marshmallow burner, or a slow roaster?"

A genuine giggle erupts from my chest. "Burner for sure. You?"

He tosses his head back, groaning. "No," he drawls. "I thought for sure you'd be a slow roaster. You know the best things in life take time."

"Do they? Doesn't seem so lately."

Leaning forward, he gives me another kiss. "You're right, not *all* things I guess."

I bite my lip to suppress the smile that forms.

Sitting in comfortable silence, we *slow* roast our marshmallows, stealing glances at each other as we take time to not burn them. When Miller finishes assembling his s'more, he holds the delicious treat near my mouth, encouraging me to take a bite since my marshmallow is still roasting.

Melted chocolate assaults my taste buds as I take it between my teeth, moaning in appreciation. Pulling my mouth away, a string of marshmallow pulls from the dessert, sticking to my chocolate covered lips and making a giant mess. His tongue comes out to steal the string of marshmallow, and he pulls it into his mouth as he takes his own full bite.

Setting the rest of his s'more down on the edge of the firepit, he kisses me, and I'm overwhelmed by the taste of chocolate and *Miller*.

I don't think I've ever tasted anything this amazing.

I melt into him as he takes the marshmallow skewer from my hand, and I assume places it on the edge of the fire, but I'm too consumed by him to look, or care, even.

Tangling his hand in my hair, we deepen the kiss, pressing our bodies against each other as he angles us, laying me against the back cushions of the outdoor couch.

Our tongues mold together, dancing seductively in a way that leaves me breathless, but it's short-lived. As Miller pulls back, he drags his tongue across my lips. "There," he repeats his actions, licking me again. "All clean."

My core throbs as he sits upright, putting some distance between us. I want to pull him back to me, but in my peripheral, something catches on fire.

"Oh, no!" Pulling the roasting stick away from the fire, it's submerged in a bright orange flame, encircling the marshmallow in black char and burning it completely.

Blowing the fire out, the smoke floats into the air, and I look over at Miller, scrunching my nose. Without hesitation, he reaches over and grabs it with two fingers, lifting away the burnt to reveal a small, perfectly melted marshmallow beneath it. He plops the char into his mouth, smiling at me as he chews. "Good as new."

Pulling the rest of the marshmallow from the skewer, its heat burns my fingertips as I feed it to him, but the heat between my legs burns hotter when Miller wraps his lips around my fingers, dragging his teeth against them as he takes the marshmallow.

My body buzzes with need, and suddenly, I couldn't care less about marshmallows, s'mores, and beachside cabanas.

The way Miller's looking at me turns my insides to Jell-O, and the only thing I want is *him*.

"Let's go," I suggest, but it definitely sounds more like a demand. He flashes me a knowing smile.

"Not in the mood for s'mores, Snow Angel?"

"Not anymore." Standing, I take his hand and tug so he'll stand, too.

"What are you in the mood for, then?" His eyes glitter with mischief, the illumination from the fire highlighting his amusement.

"You. Take me home?"

"Nah, let's go for a walk on the beach instead." Toeing off his shoes, he reaches down and pulls off his socks, then drops to his knee to remove mine.

"I...wha... Okay." It's impossible to hide my surprise, but I try to force myself to go with the flow as he pushes to a stand once I'm barefoot and grabs my hand.

Lacing our fingers together, he leads me down to the water. The further we get from the bustle of the hotel, the louder the waves become, until the only sound is them crashing against the shore.

The water is freezing as it hits my toes, and I squeak, instinctively dancing away from Miller and the frigid sea, running a few steps back to the soft sand.

To our left is a cluster of boulders, so I start to walk toward them, knowing Miller will be close behind. I only get a few steps ahead when I sense his presence, and when I peek over my shoulder, I see him stalking after me. A smile plays across his lips, looking at me like I'm his prey, which does nothing to ease the knot of arousal growing inside me.

When I reach them, I say nothing as I wait for Miller to join me, then take his hand. As we round the boulders, we're immediately out of view of everyone else.

It's quiet on this side of the beach, secluded, and completely dark aside from the lights on in the neighboring apartment complexes.

"Trying to get me alone, Snow Angel?"

"Maybe." My bare foot presses against the rough edge of a boulder, still wet from the waves that crashed against it earlier. I climb onto it and stand, looking into the black ocean.

Miller does the same as he wraps his arms around my waist. We're still out of view, the other boulders blocking us from the apartments—at least, I think.

At this point, I don't really care.

I'm burning with need for him, desperate for his touch.

Leaning against him, I feel his erection press through his jeans and against my backside, and I know he's feeling the same.

Turning my head, I lift my head, and he meets my silent request, kissing me deeply.

My entire body melts in a relaxed sigh as his hand reaches beneath my shirt, splaying across my stomach. His fingers drift lower, and he unbuttons my jeans, pushing his hand into my panties. A sharp intake of breath inundates my lungs as he touches me, circling my most sensitive spot.

"Is this too much?" he whispers, his teeth nipping at my ear.

"No. I want you. Please." My eyes flutter shut, my body acutely aware of his.

"If we do this here, there won't be anything sweet or soft about it, Snow Angel. I can't dote on you and worship your body. It'll be hard and fast. If that's not what you wa—"

"It is," I breathe, my voice raspy and almost unrecognizable to my own ears. "I need you, Miller."

"*Fuck.* Okay. Hold on to that boulder."

I do as he says, holding onto the large rock in front of me, before looking over my shoulder at him.

Miller takes his wallet out, procuring a condom before he pushes his pants down his hips just enough to pull himself out.

Sliding it down his shaft, he shoves the wrapper into his pocket, then pulls my pants down until they're around the tops of my thighs. "Tell me if it's too rough," he growls, and I lean further down.

"It won't be."

Carefully, he knocks my feet a little further apart, then aligns himself with my entrance.

We both groan as he pushes into me in one thrust, pausing to let my body accommodate. "Is this okay?"

"Yes. *God, yes.* Move, Miller," I beg, my eyes rolling back as he steadies one hand on my hip while wrapping the other around my body to reach my clit.

Obeying my wish, he begins to move, and my body succumbs to three of my most heightened senses. All I can feel is him, and all I can hear is the crashing of the waves, as he quickly makes me see stars brighter than the ones in the night sky.

The cold ocean air whips around us as Miller pounds into me, the sound of skin slapping against skin clashing with the water just a few feet below us. The ocean spray splashes around us, and somehow a chill still runs through me, even though my body is burning hot.

"Does that feel good, Snow Angel? You like feeling me deep inside you when we overlook the ocean?"

Pushing my butt back into him more, I nod my head, bringing my hand over his. "You feel so freaking good."

Miller circles my clit with his finger as he grabs my waist, his fingernails digging into my skin with every grunt that leaves his lips. From this angle, he's impossibly deep, and I feel him practically in my stomach.

On the other side of the boulders, voices draw closer, but it doesn't slow us. My fingernails bite into the top of his hand, and I turn my head, looking for the source.

"Does that turn you on, Zee? Knowing we could get

caught at any second? Your pussy just got so damn wet." He slides in and out of me excruciatingly slowly, sending sparks through veins.

"So hot," I breathe incoherently as my orgasm begins to crest. I'm so close, so incredibly close to the edge of release.

Moaning his name, my toes curl into the rough stone below them. "Miller...I'm...I'm going to..."

"I can feel it. Your body is so responsive to me, Snow Angel. Let me hear your voice merge with the waves as you scream my name."

It takes a few more circles of Miller's expert fingers before I'm falling over the edge, seeing stars as he brings me to orgasm. He must have been holding his own release off, because the second he feels my body let go, he comes too. Holding my body to his, he rests his forehead on my back as he finishes inside me.

"You're amazing, Zee. That was so sexy I'm not even sure how this is really my life right now."

"I've never done anything like that before," I admit as he pulls out and helps tug my pants back in place.

Turning to face him, he catches my lips with his as he removes the condom and tucks himself back in his jeans. "Neither have I," he smirks, tying a knot in the contraceptive, and hiding it from view in his hand, "but I definitely want to do it again sometime."

"Me too."

Carefully, we climb back down to the sand, lacing our fingers together as we start to walk back toward the hotel.

Passing a nearby trash can, he tosses the condom in, then we head back to the cabana to pick up our discarded shoes. As we put them on, I look around, feeling a little remorseful that we didn't spend more time here, and now we don't have the option.

"What should we do now?" I ask as we walk away, feeling a little bummed I didn't get to eat an entire s'more, although the alternative was just as sweet.

"Now we're going home, Snow Angel." Turning to me suddenly, he wraps his arms around the backs of my legs and tosses me over his shoulder, slapping his palm to my butt as I hang upside down. "I didn't get to worship your body, and I plan on making it up tenfold."

"Miller!" I squeal, laughing and trying to lift my upper body as he walks us to the parking lot. Bystanders look at us, a few giggling as he carries me like a Neanderthal past a line of electric cars.

"Yeah, that's what you'll be screaming later, too."

"Put me down!"

"As you wish." Smacking my butt again, he grabs a handful in his palm before he drops me to my feet on the passenger side of his truck, then presses me up against it and kisses me, making me lose my breath all over again.

Zee

Chapter Twenty

"**I** 'm so nervous," I mutter aloud as I approach the small town of San Ysabel. I'm heading back to Julian, trying to keep myself from spiraling with every mile that passes.

We've already exchanged I love you's.

And it's true. I've fallen hard and fast for Miller Ryan, and I know that with every piece of me.

But there's still so much unknown.

How will we make this work? An hour drive is significant, but not impossible.

What about in the future when we want to live together? How can I possibly ask him to give up his life in Julian...but what about mine in San Diego?

And then there's an entirely other issue at hand. *What if the Stokes family doesn't accept my apology for lying to them?*

From the backseat, Potato growls low in his small crate, drawing me from my thoughts. He hates being confined in the carrier, and hates car rides even more. I know he's going to be miserable at Miller's house for the next couple of days, but I couldn't bear the thought of leaving him again.

Originally, I only had New Year's Eve and New Year's Day off, but I was able to switch a couple of shifts and give myself a little extra time to spend in Julian with Miller.

Now, I'm on my way back up to where this all started, this time with Potato in tow. It feels like a lifetime has passed, when in reality, it's been a week.

How has my life turned upside down in just seven days?

"I know, buddy, I know. We're almost there, I promise."

No sooner do the words leave my mouth, my phone rings, blasting through the speakers and startling me. My heart beats wildly as I press the green button on my dash to answer the call.

"Hey, Gen!"

"Hey! Do you have any plans tonight? Mine fell through, so I wanted to see if you were free." Her voice fills my car, and I turn the volume down just a bit so it's not blaring.

"I'm actually almost to Julian."

"Oh! I can hear the smile in your tone, Zee. Ringing in the new year with your new beau?"

"You could say that. Going to come clean to his aunt and uncle today, and I'm a nervous wreck."

My stomach twists in knots as my car climbs further up the mountain.

"Stop. They already love you. That won't change."

"They've met me once," I stress. "They're going to be *really* pissed that I lied to them from the get-go."

"Eh." Something rustles in the background, muffling her voice a little. "Don't put words in their mouth, Zee. Just see what happens."

I sigh and glance in my rearview mirror again. "You're right."

"Typically, I am. Is that hot doctor going to be there?"

"How do you know he's hot?"

"Because you have good taste in men. You wouldn't have gone on a date with him if he wasn't attractive."

My head bobs along in agreement even though she can't see it. She's not wrong. All the men I chose for holidates were super cute. "Yes, Lincoln is supposed to be there. He's feeling just as guilty as I am about this."

"Good, place the blame on him. It was his idea. It's *his* family."

"I know, but I really care about Miller, and that's his family, too."

"Ah, Zee. Always so logical."

"So, what happened to your plans tonight?" I ask, drumming my fingers against the steering wheel.

"Killian and I broke up."

I roll my eyes. "I didn't realize you were seeing him again."

I don't know Killian, per se, but I know what she's told me about him and it's enough to make me not like him.

"*Again* being the operative word. I should've learned the first time."

"We all make mistakes."

"Yeah, well, I won't be making that one again. Fool me once, shame on you, fool me twice, shame on me, and all that."

"I'm here if you need anything."

"Technically, you're not, because I need to get drunk tonight and kiss a new prince at midnight." She laughs at herself. "Seriously though, I know you are, Zee. Thank you. Do you need me to check on Potato while you're gone?"

Smiling, I glance at him in my rearview mirror. "No, I actually brought him."

"That was rude of you. Uprooting him from his comfy home on a holiday."

"I *know*, but I wasn't sure how long I would be up here, and I didn't want to ask you to watch him without having a solid plan."

"You know I would've done it," she singsongs, seeming a little distant from her phone. She must have set it down.

"That's because you're the best."

"Speakin' the truth. Okay, well, I need to go call a few more people to see what is happening tonight. I don't really want to ring in the new year alone."

"Be safe. Let me know what you end up doing!"

"Will do, drive carefully."

"Thanks." Hanging up, I turn my attention to a very grumpy Potato in the back again. "We're almost there, buddy," I coo, hoping to bring him some comfort even though he's probably trying to think of ways to murder me in my sleep.

Up ahead, I spot the Ryan Family Tree sign, and excitement races through me. Passing the corner tree farm, I follow the GPS instructions and drive a little further, turning down an unmarked road about a quarter mile down.

The road is freshly plowed of snow, but seems to go on forever as I follow it.

Finally, the trees thin, and a quaint cabin comes into view, settled in the middle of the picturesque forest.

Smoke rises from the chimney, and Miller's red truck is parked out front. Pulling my car up beside it, I turn it off just as Miller opens the front door.

As he emerges onto his porch, I can't help but swoon as he tucks his hands into his pockets, looking every ounce the lumber snack I know him to be in his red flannel jacket with his white tee shirt underneath, his jeans, and boots.

"Hi," he says, pulling open the driver's side door. Bending at the waist, he leans in and kisses me as I unbuckle my seatbelt.

"Hey."

In the backseat, Potato lets out another low growl again.

"He pissed?" Miller glances at my cat's carrier in the backseat.

"Immensely."

"Great. I wonder how he's going to get along with Penny."

"I think it'll be best to lock him in your second bedroom. He'll probably hide most of the time anyway, but if he does venture out from under the bed, it'll be good to have him confined to one room."

"Yeah, whatever you think is best."

Grabbing my overnight bag, and the cat carrier, Miller leads us into his cabin, waiting until I'm fully in before using his boot to close the door behind us.

It's sparse, but exactly what I pictured for him. A substantial fire roars in the fireplace, filling the air with its warmth—a stark difference from the temperature outside. There's a cozy couch with a burgundy-colored blanket tossed over the top, a couple of end tables, and a flatscreen TV mounted on the wall opposite the fireplace.

As I look around and take it all in, Miller brings my belongings to the guest room. I want to explore, but follow him instead so I can get Potato set up and comfortable in his temporary environment.

"Hopefully he doesn't take too long to settle in." Miller places the carrier on top of the bed, then kisses the side of my head and leaves me to it, shutting the door quietly behind him.

The door to the cat carrier hardly swings on its hinges before Potato zooms out and hides under the guest room bed.

"You'll be safe here, big guy. This is only for a couple days." My words are spoken in vain, as not even a grumpy meow responds back.

Moving into the attached bathroom, I set up his litter

box and bowls, then put a small scratching post near the foot of the bed.

When I'm satisfied my fur baby has everything he needs, I close the door quietly behind me, and seek out Miller, finding him sitting on the couch. When he sees me, he opens his arms wide so I can sink onto his lap. My arms curl around his neck as his arms encircle my waist, and I press a soft kiss to the side of his cheek. His scruff is rough against my lips, but I pepper him in more kisses, anyway.

"Potato good?" he asks, rubbing his thumb against the small sliver of skin my shirt is exposing.

"He will be. He's hiding."

"That's good. Penny can't get in there and terrorize him, so I'm sure he'll get comfortable in no time."

"Thank you for letting me bring him."

"Of course. Anything you need."

Our lips meet in a soft kiss, which he breaks all too soon. Tucking my messy hair behind my ears, he says, "We have a few hours before we have to be at my aunt and uncles. Anything you want to do? We could go into town if you want to check it out."

"Actually, I did think of something I want to do, but it's kind of silly."

"I enjoy silly sometimes. What is it?"

Biting my lip, I try not to giggle with excitement at the thought of doing such a childish activity, but I can't help how giddy just the thought of it makes me. Looking up at him, I ask, "Do you want to build a snowman with me?"

He roars a laugh. "That's what you want to do?"

I blush, nodding enthusiastically. Even if he doesn't want to, I can still go out and do it myself. "Yes."

Grabbing my hand, he pulls us from the couch and tugs me further into his home. "Okay, if we're going to do this, we have to do it right. Tell me what you want your snowman to wear."

As I throw out ideas, he leads me down the hall, tapping his finger to his lips in thought as we set off in search of supplies.

"I think I might be sick." Shaking my hands nervously, I look over at Miller, wondering if my face reflects a shade of green since I'm feeling like I might vomit.

I'm about to come face-to-face with the family I lied to. Face-to-face with the man I *fake*-dated.

Blowing out a very shaky breath, I look out the window, my foot bouncing against the floorboard of the truck.

"It's going to be fine." Miller reaches over and squeezes my knee. "Just relax, Snow Angel."

"I just can't shake the feeling that this is all about to blow up in my face."

"I bet you'll be pleasantly surprised. Tim and Tina are reasonable people. You'll see."

"And Lincoln?"

Miller takes a right-hand turn onto his aunt and uncle's street.

"What about him?"

"What if he's decided this is too weird for him? He's had time to think. What if his fake girlfriend of *one day* dating his actual cousin is too...awkward?"

"I think you are overthinking this way too much. I promise you everything will be fine."

In the next breath, we're pulling into the familiar driveway of Tim and Tina's house, up alongside Lincoln's car. The sun is setting, darkness beginning to shroud all around us, and it feels like a warning, which doesn't give me a lot of comfort.

Coming around to my side of the truck, Miller opens my door and extends his hand, helping me hop out. He presses a chaste kiss to my lips as he closes the door, then laces his fingers with mine and leads me up the porch.

He barely lifts his hand to knock when the door is practically pulled from his hinges.

"Miller! Holly! It's so good to see you both. Please, come in, come in." Tina smooths her hands against her apron and steps aside for us to enter.

She kisses my cheek in greeting and I send a panicked look in Miller's direction before he helps me shrug out of my coat. Squeezing my hip reassuringly, he turns to his aunt and wraps her in a hug.

I'm about to explode with nerves.

"Seems like the five of us have some things to discuss!"

Tina claps her hands. "C'mon, Linc and Tim are in the living room."

A wave of guilt hits me at the mention of Lincoln's name, and as I follow her into the other room where the men are, he instantly greets me with a wide smile. Pushing up from his seat, he walks over to meet with his arms open, pulling me into a warm hug.

"Hey! You look well." He kisses me on the side of the head, like a brother would do to a sister.

Dropping my voice, I look up at him. "I need to tell them. Sooner than later."

He nods, understanding shining through his eyes. "Whenever you're ready."

"That would be never," I grumble. "But I guess now is good."

We all take a seat around the coffee table, Tina on the side of the couch closest to where Tim sits in his recliner, and Lincoln in the opposite recliner. Miller and I take the other cushions on the couch.

Despite the looks of curiosity from his aunt and uncle, Miller takes my hand again and pulls it into his lap. Our intertwined fingers rest on his thigh, and I don't miss the way Tina's gaze drops to them before she looks up at me.

Tension is thick in the air as we all sit silently, and I glance at Lincoln, hoping he'll take the lead on this.

After another heavily awkward moment, he speaks, and relief floods through me. "So, I guess you can see that Holly and I aren't together. It turns out she and Miller have something pretty special, and I couldn't be the guy to stand in their way."

Tim's gaze bounces from his son to Miller before his eyes connect with mine. He says nothing, though, and instead turns to his wife. Tina wears a blank expression, which is strange to see on her. Usually so enthusiastic, right now she's being quiet and reserved.

"I never came here and expected to meet someone who instantly captured my interest." I swallow the lump in my throat as my heart threatens to combust in my chest. I feel physically sick. Terrified of what they'll think of me after this. "Meeting Miller was a coincidence. I had no idea he owned the tree farm when I walked over to it, let alone was related to Lincoln. I thought he was just some nice guy who helped ice my ankle after I embarrassed myself. I was completely caught off guard when he walked in on Christmas morning."

"How do you feel about this?" Tina asks Lincoln. There's a slight bite to her tone that makes me want to cave in on myself.

Lincoln glances down at his lap before looking back at his mother. "Holly and I were actually never together, Mom. In fact, we didn't even know each other prior to Christmas Eve."

My heart twists as I add, "And my name isn't Holly. It's Elizabeth. Zee for short."

"I don't understand." Tina's face contorts with confusion.

"Your name isn't Holly?" Tim chimes in. "Why would you give us a fake name?"

"Because this was never supposed to be more than a one-time meeting. I met Lincoln through a dating app called SparksFly after I created a profile so I could set up a few holiday dates throughout the month." My eyes meet his for a second before I drop them back to my lap. Miller squeezes my hand, encouraging me to continue. "Lincoln reached out and asked if I would join him for Christmas Eve dinner. We met for coffee that morning so that we weren't complete strangers upon coming here."

"None of this makes any sense to me," Tina says with sadness. "Why lie?" But that question isn't directed at me. She's looking at Lincoln.

He sighs, and I can tell he's struggling with what he wants to say to his parents. "I've worked really hard through med school and working my way up at the hospital. I guess I just couldn't take another holiday where the main point of topic was when I would meet someone and settle down. Holly—*Elizabeth*—presented as the perfect cover. It was purely by chance that I found her profile that night, and I don't regret having her come for Christmas Eve. If I hadn't, she wouldn't have met Miller, and that dopey grin on his face hasn't left since he met her."

"I've fallen in love with her," Miller asserts, scooting closer to the edge of the couch. He reaches over me and grabs his aunt's hand. "Please don't be angry at Zee for all of this."

"I'm not angry," Tina shoots back, definitely

sounding angry. "I'm just so confused. Lincoln, why would you not just ask us to stop bringing up when you might settle down? We love you. We just want to see you happy."

"I hate disappointing you, and every time I had to tell you I was still single, it felt like I was doing exactly that. It's clear you're ready for grandchildren, but that's just not where I'm at this point in my life. I'm focusing on my career and myself. If I meet someone, then the rest will work itself out in due time."

"So your name is Elizabeth?" Tim asks, still trying to get up to speed, completely ignoring everything his son just said.

"Yes." My voice comes out small and timid.

I hate that I feel so hesitant around these people who have been nothing but kind to me. But, like Lincoln, I'm finding their disappointment to be utterly heart-wrenching.

"And you set up a dating profile under a fake name, so you could go on dates with multiple men."

I wince. When he says it like *that*, it sounds so much worse than it is. "Yes, but it's not like what you're thinking it is. All the dates knew they were nothing more than a holidate. I was simply a companion for their holiday parties."

"Why would you want to do that, sweetheart?" Tina asks in a motherly tone.

I want to answer her, but words feel like sandpaper on my tongue. Opening and closing my mouth a couple times, I end up looking down into my lap, embarrassed and overwhelmed. "I... Because... I just..."

"Because her entire family died over the summer and she didn't want to be alone for the holidays," Miller says with frustration, scrubbing his palm down his face.

His words hang in the air, and I look at him, horror-struck. It feels like Miller just carved into my heart with a searing hot knife, slashing through it until he met the weakest spot. My family's faces flit through my mind, and I suck in a sharp breath, finding it hard to breathe.

He knows I didn't want to tell them that yet.

Tears spring to my eyes, my heart shattering into pieces, and immediately Miller realizes what he's said.

His eyes widen. "Zee, I'm so—"

"I need some air," I interrupt, jumping to my feet. "I'm sorry. I just need some air."

Rushing from the living room, I pull my coat from the coatrack, swinging it over my shoulders as I race through the door. It slams shut behind me, the *thud* echoing into the quiet winter night.

Power walking down the driveway, I hang a left when I reach the end and walk up the road, needing to clear my head. Tears cascade down my cheeks as I let my feet guide me to nowhere in particular.

It's not that I didn't want the Stokes family to understand why I did what I did. I planned on telling them eventually, or maybe even explaining it to them tonight, in my own way.

But instead, Miller let the words slip from his mouth.

When I finally pay attention to my surroundings, I'm not surprised to find I'm back at the farm, standing under the Ryan Family Tree Farm sign. With a heavy heart, I stare at Miller's last name, wondering how this last week of my life became so crazy.

There's a thick chain around the gate and I can't get in, so instead, I take a seat on the stump next to it, resting my elbows on my knees as I lean my head into my hands. I just need a minute, then I'll go back.

I replay everything in my head, picturing the look on Tina's face and the confusion on Tim's. This family has been nothing but good to me, and I feel like the worst person in the world for deceiving them.

How could Miller tell them about my family?

It was an accident. I try to reason with myself. *He didn't mean to tell them when I wasn't ready.*

My tears continue to fall, the wind cold against them, causing a shiver to run through me. My nose is frozen and runny, thanks to the waterfall of tears I've cried.

The sound of footsteps crunching in the snow alerts me to someone else's presence, and as I look up, I see Miller approaching. His hands are in his pockets, and he walks closer with tentative steps, probably trying to gauge how upset I am.

When he reaches me, he drops to his knees in the snow and grabs my face with his glove-covered hands. "I'm so sorry, I overstepped. I fucked up. I'm so sorry." He kisses me urgently, then pulls back and continues to apologize. "I didn't mean to. It just slipped out. I wanted them to understand." His kisses are frantic, and this time I can't tell if the tears are coming from me or him. "Can you forgive me, Snow Angel? *Please.* I'm so sorry."

"I just feel like such a horrible person," I sob, and he pulls me closer in his arms.

"You're not."

"But I'm a liar. Do they hate me?"

"No, of course they don't hate you."

"Did you tell them the whole story?" My heart sinks as I ask. Part of me hopes he did, so I won't have to relive it, but the other part fears their pity. I don't want them to forgive me based on guilt about what happened to my family.

"I did. I had to, Zee. I'm sorry. After you left, the three of them were throwing questions at me faster than I could keep up, so I explained everything. They're worried about you, but they know not to ask you about it. They'll wait till you're ready to tell them."

"They don't hate me?" I repeat my earlier question, my brain unable to focus on anything else or move past the agonizing thought of them being mad at me.

Miller squeezes my hands and dips his head until he's in my line of vision, forcing me to look at him. "No Elizabeth, they don't hate you. They're just worried and they're trying to understand."

"Okay." I nod my head, listening to his words as he brushes the tears from my cheeks. "Okay, that's good."

Miller and I stay in this position until I start to relax more. It takes a few minutes for my heart rate to return to almost normal, and I feel like I can breathe again. He gives me the time I need, and doesn't try to move or rise from where he kneels, even though I know the snow has soaked his pants.

When I finally look at him without tears in my eyes, he squeezes my hands again. "It's freezing cold out here. Want to go in the tent to warm up?"

I shake my head, letting out a small laugh. "No, that's okay. Wouldn't want to knock down any more trees."

"Probably a good choice. I'm not sure anymore of my firs can take a beating. They're already looking a little rough this many days after Christmas." His hand reaches up to brush my cheek. "Do you want to go back to the house?"

I shake my head again, looking past him at the snow that begins to fall. "I don't think I'm ready. I just feel like such an imposter. Part of me wants to go back, and hope for the best. But the other half of me wants to run away to your cabin and hide."

"We can do that, if you want. Potato would probably be happy."

Just then, the sound of snow crunching beneath footsteps draws both of our attention. Behind us, Tim, Tina, and Lincoln come into view.

Standing, I thrust my hands in the pockets of my coat, absolutely mortified that they've all followed me out here in the cold.

"It's freezing out here," Tim comments and gestures with his chin toward the tent. "Should we go in there?"

Miller shakes his head at the same time Tina turns toward me. "I'm sorry about your family, sweetheart, and I'm sorry that Miller told us when you didn't want him to. It's your story to tell, and although his intentions were good, he took that from you. I know he feels terrible." She glances at him, then connects her eyes back with mine. "Now, Tim and I aren't fond of being deceived, but we understand why this all happened. We've already apologized to Lincoln, and now we would like to apologize to you."

"Apologize to me? For what? I'm the one who lied." I'm flabbergasted, and confused as to why they think I need an apology.

She gives me a small smile and takes a step closer. "I want to apologize for not following my intuition. When you came to us, I knew something was wrong, but I didn't press you. How could I when you had just met us? But I wish I could go back to Christmas Eve, and try to get you to open up to me, even just a little. I feel as though your soul needed that, and I ignored my gut and gave you space. If I could do it again, I would give you the comfort that I know you needed on that day."

There's no way to avoid the tears that spring back to my eyes with Tina's words. I begin to sob. "I'm so sorry. I regret everything."

"Well, I don't," Lincoln chimes in. From over his mother's shoulder, I look at him. There's a small smile on his lips as he says, "How could I when it brought you into the family?"

"He's right, Zee. I'd have you lie over and over again if that meant I still got to meet you." Miller pulls me from Tina and into his arms. Kissing me, his hand cups the back of my neck, and he deepens it slightly. When he pulls away, he rests his forehead against mine. "I love you so much."

Coming up beside me, Tina loops her arm through mine. "Come on, it's way too cold out here. Let's go back to the house and have something warm to drink until dinner is ready."

She doesn't take no for an answer and begins to lead us back with the men trailing behind. Tina begins to talk about dinner, explaining what she's made, and gushing over how her best friend gave her the recipe and that she's been so excited to try it.

She continues on with her story until she's done and nudges me with her elbow, sneaking a glance at me as we draw closer to her home. "You know, Zee, you're the gift we all asked Santa for. Some of us were just more silent than others, but we all asked, just the same. I'm so glad you're now a part of our family. I hope you'll stick around."

With tears pricking my eyes, I turn and look over my shoulder at Miller, locking eyes with the man who has stolen my heart quicker than I thought possible. He mouths *I love you*, and for the first time since losing my family, I don't feel so alone.

Zee

Epilogue

Christmas, One Year Later

"All right, time for you to open another!" Tim says, passing me a present. The thin box is wrapped in brown paper, tied with a hunter green velvet bow.

This year, the Stokes family decided to try something new, and instead of having a free-for-all when opening gifts, we're slowing down a little, taking turns to open them one at a time. Plus, it feels different without Lincoln here since he got stuck at work and wasn't able to make it.

"Me? I just opened one! It's Miller's turn." Placing my gift on the coffee table in front of me, I reach for the one I've brought for Miller, handing him the small box. He takes it from me, shaking it with a smile on his face.

"Hmm. What could this be?" he probes, shaking it again.

I shrug, trying to not give anything away with my expression. "Open it."

Sneaking a glance at Tina, she beams at me, already knowing what's inside. I told her this morning when I helped her put breakfast in the oven—an egg casserole that we made the most delicious breakfast burritos with.

Keeping up with his family's tradition, Miller and I came over first thing this morning. We were earlier than the Stokes expected us, thanks to Potato and his hungry belly deciding to beat me up the moment the sun peeked over the horizon.

Unwrapping the box, Miller tosses the paper to the side, and lifts the top. I wait with bated breath, antsy for him to figure out what it is. His brows pull together, confusion etching itself deep in his features, just as I had hoped.

Searching for the perfect gift for him was like finding a needle in a haystack. Anything he wants, he buys. There's nothing he *needs*. But there has been one thing he's been asking for, and after months of telling him the timing wasn't right, I finally felt deep in my soul that *now* is the perfect time.

Placing the box on his lap, he reaches inside, grabbing a fistful of the shredded paper. He glances up at me as he holds it in his hand, then lets it go as a smile plays on his lips. The paper floats down into the box, joining the rest of the shreds. "I'm all for creativity, but I'm not quite sure what I'm looking at here."

"Not even a small clue?" I ask playfully.

"Nope. Kindling is the only thing that comes to mind."

"That's my lease agreement."

"Okay?"

"My landlord let me out of my lease early."

His eyes widen. "Elizabeth, what are you saying right now?"

Standing, I go to where he's sitting and drop to my knees, grabbing his hands as I look up at him. *I love this man so much.* "What I'm saying is I will move in with you."

Instantly, we're both on our feet and he picks me up in a bear hug, spinning me around with excitement. I giggle as he asks with disbelief, "But what about your job?"

"I'm getting transferred to the East County location! It just got approved, so I'll have to switch back and forth between locations for the next month, but once I'm there permanently, I'll commute from here."

"You'd do that for me?"

"I'd do anything for you."

He smashes his lips to mine, then places me on my feet again. "Good, because I have one last gift for you."

"Miller! You've already given me plenty."

He shrugs. "One more."

From across the room, Tina squeals and kicks her feet against the carpet, and Tim shushes her. Glancing at them over my shoulder skeptically, I quirk a brow in a silent question. Both of them clamp their lips closed, mirroring each other in a very husband-wife way as they try to look at me innocently.

When I turn back around, my gaze instantly drops, and I suck in a sharp breath. Miller is down on one knee looking up at me with so much love in his eyes, and a ring box in his hand.

"Elizabeth Ashford. One year ago, you walked onto my farm and completely uprooted my boring, mundane life. I hadn't realized there was so much lacking until you brought so much happiness, love, and laughter into it. You've added nothing but joy to this family, and effortlessly became one of us, as though you always belonged. I knew from the moment I saw you that you would be my wife one day, and I think I've been a pretty patient man by giving this relationship a little more time to grow since we started off as such a whirlwind. But, Zee, I can't wait any longer. Will you do me the honor of making me the happiest man alive and be my wife?"

My hand flies to my mouth, and I try my hardest not to cry, even though I know this time, they'll be happy tears. "You want me to marry you?"

"Oh, Elizabeth, I don't want you to marry me. I want you to spend your life with me, be the mother of my children, and grow old with me."

Pulling him to his feet, I toss my arms around his neck as I jump up and latch my legs around his waist. "Yes! I'll be your wife!"

Tina and Tim get to their feet in excitement, hooting and hollering, and hugging each other, as Miller spins me around again. When he places me back on my feet, his hand cradles my lower back as he dips me, and kisses me deeply.

Tim whistles low, but I ignore everyone else in the room, getting lost in my *fiancé*.

I thought nothing could top last Christmas when I met and fell in love with the man of my dreams, but I'll never forget this moment.

Miller kisses me like I am the answer to all of his prayers, but what he doesn't realize is that he's the answer to mine.

Before him, I let the loneliness and the grief of losing my family consume me. But now…now I feel whole again. And although I'll never stop missing my parents and brother, part of my heart will always feel full thanks to the everlasting Christmas gift the Stokes family and Miller have given me.

When the Christmas festivities have winded down, and Tim and Tina retire to their bedroom, Miller and I sit in front of the crackling fire in comfortable silence.

With my head resting against Miller's chest and my feet curled under me, I could fall asleep. And the way he's rhythmically rubbing his fingertips against my arm makes me think he wants me to.

My eyes grow heavy, and I yawn, unable to stop it from happening.

"Ready to go home?" Miller asks.

Home.

Home is where Potato is, and my heart swells, knowing he's at Miller's cabin.

My head bobs in a nod. "Yes."

Pushing to his feet, Miller stands, tugging me with him. He wraps his arm around my shoulders, and leads me to the door. Stopping to put on our coats, he tugs my beanie down around my ears before kissing me on the nose.

"Thank you, fiancé." I grin.

"You're welcome, fiancée."

After locking up behind us, Miller cranks the heater in the truck for me, and drives us back to his cabin. I spend the short ride admiring my sparkling diamond ring, and it shimmers under every streetlight we pass under. "It's beautiful. I can't believe I'm going to be your wife."

"I can. I knew you would be from the moment I saw you, remember?" He glances over at me, grinning.

"So I'm thinking I'll move up here during the last week of January. I have my apartment until January thirtieth, and I transfer to the East County location on January twenty-seventh."

"Whenever you want, Snow Angel. I'd keep you here now if I could."

"Do you think Potato and Penny will ever get along?"

"That depends on if Potato ever decides to come out from under the bed."

There have been numerous occasions over the last year that I've brought Potato with me to Miller's and each time, he's never ventured further than his food bowls.

We've tried everything to coax him out from under the guest bed, but we're always unsuccessful.

"Highly unlikely then." I laugh as Miller pulls in front of his cabin. Cutting the engine, he hops out of his truck and comes around to open my door. Extending his hand like he always does, he helps me down and laces our fingers together as we walk to the house.

Once inside, he flips the light switch, casting a warm glow throughout the living room.

"Penny," he calls out, looking for his dog. It's unusual she's not right at the door waiting for us.

Moving further into the house, he calls for her again, and I start to look around, wondering where she could be. "Did she sneak out the back?" I ask, but as I peer into the kitchen, I see the backdoor closed and locked.

"Penny! C'mere girl!"

Moments later, I hear Miller roar a laugh. "Zee! Get in here, quick."

Racing down the hallway, I come to a stop in front of the guest bedroom, where Miller stands in the doorway. "What, what's wrong?" I asked, panicking as he blocks my view.

My heart sinks, thinking the absolute worst.

But when he steps aside so I can see, my heart swells with excitement.

On the guest bed, up by the pillows, are Penny and Potato, snuggling together in perfect contentment, like they've always been best friends. Penny's curled up in a ball, while Potato lays against her stomach like her little spoon.

"Looks like he came out from under the bed," Miller muses, leaning against the doorway and putting his arm around me.

Resting my head against his shoulder, I look at the two furry babies who I love so much, sound asleep together. There's a smile on my face as I wrap my arms around Miller's waist and confirm what we both already know. "Best Christmas ever."

Can't get enough of the holidays?
Lincoln & Genesis' story is coming 2025.
Preorder Today!

A.R. ROSE

Okay, I don't know about you but I'm still on cuteness overload after Zee & Miller's story! And we can't forget about the real star of the show, Potato.

Thank you so much to every single reader who has taken their time to read my books. I owe this entire journey to you, and I am so grateful you picked up one of my titles.

As always, I'd like to thank my team of alpha readers, Delynda, Cassie, and Ellyn, and my beta readers Megan, Kendra, and Manda. To my amazing editor, Virginia Tesi Carey, thank you for always putting up with my crazy, and to Amanda for proofreading this story! Thank you to my agent, Dani, for encouraging me to pivot to a Christmas book. Without your guidance, I would have sat on this idea for another year or more.

A special shout out to all of my readers who live in San Diego - this book was for you!

To my husband, kiddos, and family - thank you for always supporting me and my writing. You guys mean the world to me.

And finally, an extra special thank you to all ARC

readers and influencers on my team who always show their love and support.

A.R. Rose's greatest job in life is being a mom to her two boys. She is a born and raised California native who loves to hang out at home with her kids and her dog.

A.R. realized her passion for writing in the third grade, although it wasn't until early 2022 when she began to pursue it. Now, if she skips a day of writing, she feels as though her day is incomplete.

On any given day, you will find A.R. toting around her laptop and her Kindle, with a coffee in hand, daydreaming about the characters and worlds she's building. She is grateful to have the opportunity to bring her stories to life and is excited about her journey as a romance writer.

CONNECT

Join A.R. Rose's newsletter for info & updates

https://www.authorarrose.com/email-subscribe

Website

www.authorarrose.com

Reading Group

https://www.facebook.com/groups/authorarrose

Facebook

https://www.facebook.com/authorarrose

TikTok

https://www.tiktok.com/@authorarrose

Instagram

https://www.instagram.com/authorarrose

CHAPTER ONE

Age 9, Verona, Italy

"Papà! Mamma!"

The shrill sound of my six-year-old brother's laughter rises through the fragrant air as we run around my parents, playing a game of tag in the kitchen while my mother cooks. Mio padre sits at our kitchen table rubbing his temples as we race around him, my brother completely oblivious of the irritation that permeates off our father.

Tossing my hand out, I whip my fingers against his arm, just barely ghosting him as he lunges forward to avoid my touch.

"Ugh, Giulio! Sei un imbroglione!" *You're a cheater.*

He laughs again and keeps running, tripping over Mamma's feet. As he goes flying, skidding across the floor, she wags her finger at him. "I've told you the kitchen is not for playing, Giulio."

My brother stands and starts to run again until Papà stops him in his tracks.

"Enough!" Papà's voice booms as his fists hit the table. "My head is pounding, and your mother is cooking. Find somewhere else to play."

Papà is a doctor. A world-renowned surgeon, I've heard Mamma say. He works at the hospital that my bisnonno founded, and my nonno was a surgeon before my father. Nonno died when I was five, but his picture still hangs in the lobby of the hospital, alongside bisnonnos, and mio padres. Three generations of Lucchettis as doctors. *Surgeons.*

Papà says he looks forward to me becoming one, too.

Turning to my mother, his gaze softens as it lands on her. "Mia mogile, we have staff who can prepare the meals. You should be resting."

His gaze falls to where her hand rests on her stomach, rubbing where my youngest brother grows. "I love to cook, Antonio. You know this."

"Sì, bellissima. And you are so good at it. But your doctor—"

"Shh, shh. I know my body, and I will rest when it tells me to."

"C'mon, Sly, let's go upstairs!" Guilio pulls my attention from our parents as he retreats from the kitchen, his small, chubby hand beckoning for me to follow.

"No, grazie, I want to draw again." Taking the seat opposite my father, I pick up my charcoal and pull my sketch pad toward me, resuming the drawing I was working on before we started our game. I've always loved to sketch, and Mamma says I've been improving greatly.

Our black lab, Polpetta, is the perfect muse for me to practice. Mamma and Papà got her when I was two, and they say my favorite food was meatballs then, so the name stuck. Nowadays, she's old and lazy, looking as round as the food she is named after.

"It's looking well," Papà compliments as he watches me shadow the outline of her nose.

"Grazie, Papà."

A loud, abrupt ringing makes me jump, shifting my charcoal into a harsh line against my page. Frowning, I look at the mistake, my shoulders sagging in defeat.

"Pronto?" my mother singsongs into the telephone. The room falls silent as my father watches with intent while she nods her head, her hand flying over her mouth as she looks at my father. Pulling the phone away from her ear, she holds it out, signaling for him to come take it from her. "It's Gabriele."

My eyes perk up at the mention of Uncle Gabriele. He lives in America, in a city full of skyscrapers and twinkling lights. The photos he brought during his last visit were magnifico, and I long to go see it for myself.

I also wish to see my cousin Lorenzo, who is the same age as I am. It makes me sad that my best friend and play-mate is across the ocean, and even though I ask a lot, Mamma and Papà still have not taken me and Giulio to see them.

"Gabriele," my father barks into the phone. "What is it this time?"

My father's expression morphs from irritated to infuriated, his golden-bronze skin turning red from his neck through his face.

"HOW?" he shouts, his eyes darting to Mamma before he lowers his tone. "How could you get yourself into *that* much trouble, Gabriele? I—no. *No.* Absolutely not."

He turns his back, cupping his hand over the place where he speaks as though to shield his words. I don't hear what he says before he slams the phone into where it rests on the wall.

"Sylvester, go to your room, please. Mamma and I need to speak alone." I can hear the anger in his tone, see the quake in his shoulders, but he doesn't look over at me as he commands my instructions. I know better than to argue, so I collect my sketchbook and shuffle out of the kitchen without a word.

For the next two hours, me and Guilio sit at the top of our home's staircase, listening to Mamma and Papà argue. The sounds of heightened yet muffled voices and Mamma's anguished sobs traveling through the polished surfaces of our house.

One of our housemaids tried to shoo us back to our bedrooms an hour ago, but instead, I tucked my younger brother under my arm and stayed put. We can't hear what our parents speak of, but a twisting in my stomach tells me nothing good will come of it.

- - -

A gulp of saliva catches in my throat as I tilt my head back and look at the giant stone mansion. Mamma tucks my hand into hers, ushering Guilio and me away from the car that brought us here while it idles against the curb.

"Boys, you are to be on your best behavior. This is a business visit for your Papà and Uncle Gabriele. You are to be seen and not heard—it is of much importance. Do you understand me?"

"Sì, Mamma," I answer for both of us.

It has been one week since we moved to America, and three weeks since the phone call from Uncle Gabriele that changed everything for our family.

That very same night Guilio and I listened to Mamma and Papà argue—they came into our rooms and told us Uncle Gabriele needed his family close and we would be moving to New York.

Eavesdropping on several of Papà's phone calls taught me Uncle Gabriele made some bad decisions and owed someone a lot of money. And if they didn't get it, they would do very bad things to him.

I still don't understand why we had to leave our country to go help him, but at least I get to see Lorenzo more.

The steps leading up to the house make me feel like I am climbing a mountain. The stone clicks beneath Mamma's pointy shoes and I look down at them for distraction. My heart races, and Papà's hand engulfs my shoulder as he comes to stand behind me while we wait for the door to be answered. Uncle Gabriele stands to his right, fidgeting, while Aunt Andrea squats to smooth the front of Lorenzo's jacket.

When the door opens, a tall man wearing a suit greets us with an unfriendly look on his face. Beyond him, I take in the elegance of the house. Shiny marble floors, a grand staircase, sculptures and artwork—this place could be a museum.

"Come in," the man says simply, then steps aside while holding the door.

I hear my uncle clear his throat as Mamma steps forward with me and my brother in tow. Once inside, a line of women in plain dresses stand, and one rushes to my mother.

Once the door closes, the loudness of the city disappears, and a cold silence takes its place.

"May I take your coat, ma'am?"

"Yes, grazie," she says, letting go of our hands to shrug out of her coat. Papà steps forward to help before removing his own and hands both to the lady waiting.

"Gabriele," a man says as he steps out of a nearby room. His hands are in the pockets of his pants as he moves slowly toward us, his eyes glued to my uncle. He walks like a hungry lion stalking a gazelle.

He looks mean. Scary.

Is this the man who is mad at my uncle? If he is, why are we here, at his house?

"Maurizio." My uncle's head dips as though he's

bowing. "Thank you for having my family at your lovely home. This is my beautiful wife, Andrea, and son Lorenzo. As well as my brother, Antonio, and his family."

Giulio shuffles sideways until he's hidden behind Mamma's legs, but I stand straighter and move my shoulders back, trying not to seem as small as I feel.

The man my uncle introduced us to looks at us each and hums, scrunching his lips as he rubs his well-groomed beard.

My father clears his throat and takes a step forward, his hand extended. "Pleased to meet you, amico mio. Thank you for having us."

"I wasn't aware there was an *us* attending when I extended the invitation to Gabriele, but alas, our staff has prepared a large meal. We may as well break bread." He never takes Papà's hand.

I watch my father's eyes narrow before he quickly stows the look away and masks it with a smile. "I see. Well, I hope there is no trouble."

"Not at all," Maurizio clips and turns to one of the women standing along the wall. "Please see to it that the kitchen places...seven additional seats at the table."

"Certainly, Mr. Paladino." She practically runs through a set of doors just a few steps away.

The man turns to my mother and aunt, his tone softening as he speaks to them. "My wife, Leighton, should be down with our daughter any minute. You can wait in the sitting room while I take the men to my office. Should you need anything, Capaul can assist you."

"Thank you, Mr. Paladino," Aunt Andrea says as she ushers Lorenzo through the archway in the wall and into the room to our left. Mamma does the same, steering Giulio and me right behind her.

The room is bright from the sun, with plush couches and fluffy pillows, and a small table with a neat pile of children's books and grown-up magazines. It looks fancy, and immediately I am afraid to dirty it and get in trouble.

Lorenzo, on the other hand, takes a running leap onto the light gray sofa across the room, landing with a soft thud face down. His laugh is muffled as his mother scolds him.

"Enzo!" she hisses. "This is not the place for jokes!" Pulling him up, she pushes his small body until he's sitting on the couch as he should be.

Mamma's hand on my back urges me forward, and I sit on the bigger of the two couches as she and Giulio do the same. Handing us both a book, she passes another to my cousin. "Read these, boys. And keep quiet until we tell you otherwise. *Please*, behave." She shares a look with my aunt before I look down at my book.

The Giving Tree by Shel Silverstein.

I huff out an annoyed breath, not wanting to read this dumb book again but knowing if I don't, Mamma will be angry. The book is made for little kids, and I'm *nine*. But Mamma says the best way to practice my second language is through repetition.

Staring at the pages without reading the words, we wait in the room for what feels like forever. Mamma and

Aunt Andrea keep sharing looks. Guilio gets restless, sliding off the couch and onto the floor to crawl under the table. I sneak a peek at Enzo and see that he looks as though he's about to fall asleep with his arm propped up on the side of the couch.

What is taking so long?

More long minutes pass before the sound of footsteps pulls my attention and I glue my eyes to what I can see of the hallway. Moments later, a lady and a girl appear, both with smiles on their faces.

The girl looks to be about my age. She wears a puffy pink dress and her dark brown hair is long. I wonder if she has any brothers for me to play with.

Mamma and Aunt Andrea stand. Should I?

"Hello, ladies. Boys," the lady greets happily, walking over to us.

Sliding off the couch, I stand close to Mamma as the lady approaches and reaches for her hands.

"It's so nice to meet you! I'm Leighton, and this is my daughter, Vincenza. Come here, Vincenza."

The girl bounces over to her mother and waves at mine.

"I wasn't aware Gabriele was bringing his whole family for his meeting with my husband, or I never would have let my father take our boys this week for a hunting trip! They would have loved more little boys to play with."

"That's alright," Mamma affirms. "It seems as though our presence was a bit of a surprise. My name is Valentina, and these are my sons Sylvester and Giulio."

Aunt Andrea steps forward and extends a hand to shake with the lady, Lee-something. "Thank you for having us in your gorgeous home. I'm Andrea, Gabriele's wife. And this is our son Lorenzo."

"Ah, yes. I've met Gabriele a few times now! So nice to finally meet you." She gestures for everyone to sit, so we do, and she takes a seat in the armchair across from us. The girl settles on the floor by her mother's side with a chapter book on her lap.

"How old are your boys?" Aunt Andrea asks as she places her hand on Enzo's knee to keep him from wiggling.

"Luciano, my oldest, is fourteen. Then we have Joseph, who is eleven, Vincenza here, just turned nine, and Samuele, my baby, is four." She sighs. "They just grow so quickly. I can't believe I have a teenager." Looking over at my mother, she squeals, "And you! Look at that baby bump! When are you due?"

"Federico will be arriving in three to four months. Lord never knows with my boys, they come when they please. Sylvester was nearly two weeks late, but Giulio was a month early. I've stopped trying to guess when the Lucchetti boys may arrive." My eyes trace where my mother rubs my baby brother in her stomach, and she smiles warmly at me. "Sly is nine, Giulio is six."

"Oh, I understand that, honey. My kids were all over the place too." She smiles warmly at Enzo. "And you, sir? How old are you?"

Enzo shifts in his seat, sitting up taller as he proudly boasts, "I'm about to turn ten!"

"Such a little man you are!" Lee-whatever says affectionately.

Her sentence is barely finished when a woman wearing the same plain dress as all the other maids comes into the room.

"Your presence is requested in the dining room," she tells us and curtsies low before leaving.

It's very strange.

The grown-ups stand and Mamma pulls Giulio to his feet before we follow the lady out of the room. I watch as the girl bounces on her feet, skipping and twirling the whole way across the hall.

She's odd. So bouncy, and why is her dress so big?

When we enter through the open double doors of the dining room, Papà, Uncle Gabriele, and the scary man are already sitting at the table. They stand when they see us, and I follow Mamma over to the side where Papà sits.

She settles us, and once the room grows still, the scary man stands and clinks a knife against his short glass filled with a dark-golden liquid.

"I find myself to be a reasonable man. A *family* man. Which is why I'd like to welcome you all to my home this evening for dinner. Though unplanned, it seems fitting, as I have recently learned that things don't always go *as planned.* I hope that through this act of breaking bread and sharing time, minds will change before the night is over." His words trail off as he stares at my uncle, who I see gulp, the knob in his throat moving. "Now, please join me in prayer. Dear Heavenly Father, we ask that you bless our food and the guests we have here tonight to share it. May you offer your wisdom and guidance to those who may need it the most, and that you share your light by blessing our families, cultivating our relationships, and nurturing our businesses. In Jesus' name, Amen."

"Amen," I whisper, as everyone joins in.

Mamma and Papà exchange a look right before the sound of a loud snap echoes through the room.

With it, four people in black clothes walk forward and reach between us, pulling the shiny silver tops off the food sitting in the middle of the table.

Immediately, several scents hit me, and my stomach growls. Roasted chicken, steak, capellini pasta with Alfredo sauce, penne marinara, and fresh baked bread. My eyes bounce from dish to dish, skipping quickly over anything green—Mamma will make me eat my vegetables, but that doesn't mean I have to look forward to them.

With the clatter of dishes around us, I hear Mamma whisper to Papà, "Cosa significa che spera che le menti cambiano?" *What does he mean he hopes minds will change?*

"Shh, shh," Papà whispers, before painting on a smile and turning to the head of the table. "Everything looks delizioso, Maurizio. Grazie."

The scary man, Maurizio, begins to serve himself, and as soon as his wife does, the rest of the adults do the same.

When our plates and our mouths are full, I realize no one is speaking. A rarity for a meal with my family.

Looking around the table, I see the scary man sending

mean looks in my uncle's direction, while his wife fusses over the girl, trying to get her to try the food on her plate.

I don't know why she wouldn't want to.

Shoveling my mouth full bite after bite, I clear my plate and lean back in my chair, my stomach protruding.

"That was delizioso!" I exclaim loudly, knowing I was to be seen and not heard tonight, but not liking the silence. We speak at dinner. Why is no one speaking?

The scary man turns his attention to me, and suddenly I wish I had kept quiet. I am surprised when his grumpy look wipes clean. "I am glad, piccolo Lucchetti."

His gaze sweeps along the table, and he turns to his wife. "Leighton, my dear, perhaps now that we have finished, the men can speak once more?"

"Sure, my love," she tells him, then leans over to kiss him—*ew*. "Ladies, kiddos, shall we?"

Standing, she helps her daughter pull out her chair while Mamma and Aunt Andrea help us. Mamma casts another look to Papà, who nods, and Aunt Andrea bends to kiss Uncle Gabriele.

Why is everyone kissing?

As we walk away, I slow my steps to eavesdrop. "Have you thought about my offer, Gabriele?"

"Maurizio, *please*, there must be another way I can—"

"You have stolen from me, Gabriele! I have given more than enough time and patience because at one time I called you my most loyal employee, but *now* I need an answer. Have we come to an understanding?"

I look over my shoulder in time to see my uncle shake

his head no, and watch as the scary man stands, forcing my uncle to look up at him. "How disappointing. You abuse my patience, even after I am gracious enough to take in your family for a meal."

My mother turns and sees that I have completely stopped walking, and hurries back to grab my arm. As she pulls me toward the door, the scary man continues yelling at my uncle, without actually raising his voice. "I put my trust in you, Gabriele. It was misguided, and it won't be forgotten. Let this be a warning to you, Antonio, of what happens when you cross Maurizio Paladino." Maurizio's gaze lifts and he watches us as we near the door.

We hardly cross the threshold before their butler pulls both doors closed behind us, slamming them shut. They hardly click into place when the piercing sound of a gunshot rings out behind them.

"NO!" Aunt Andrea screams, charging toward the door, but the man blocking it holds her back.

The girl, Vincenza, whimpers at the sound and curls into her mother, burying her head into the fabric of her dress. Her mother's hand covers her own mouth as though she's surprised.

"I'm so sorry," she cries out, but she's already pushing her daughter down the hall and away from us.

They disappear quickly as Mamma rushes to Aunt Andrea, pulling her into her arms while she sobs louder than I've ever heard anyone cry before.

Seconds later the doorknobs twist loudly, and Papà

appears, tossing open the doors and stepping through them. His eyes are wild and fearful as he looks at each one of us. "Come," he says hurriedly. "We must leave. *Now.*"

His eyes zero in on mine, speaking what he cannot say aloud. I nod in a silent understanding and grab the hands of my brother and my cousin, and pull them to the front door. Papà's footsteps are heavy behind mine as he guides Mamma and Aunt Andrea, leaning around me to open the front door when we reach it.

Once we're in the town car again, and our driver has made it safely away from the Paladino home, does the reality of what happened sink in.

Everything happened so quickly, and if I thought our lives were turned upside down before, I have a feeling I am sadly mistaken.

Aunt Andrea's loud sobs have turned into breathless hysteria as she cries into Mamma's bosom. Lorenzo is curled up on the seat, folded into himself with his head on his mother's lap. I can't tell if he's crying.

Papà hands Giulio his activity pack he brings with him on car rides to keep him occupied before looking at me.

It's then I see smatters of blood across his white starched shirt. My stomach dips and I look away, out the window.

The city lights are bright, even through the darkened tint of the car, and it's only when the traffic begins to move and the lights begin to blur, do I allow a quiet stream of tears to fall.

There are two things I learned for certain today.

One: My uncle is dead.

And two: Never trust a Paladino.

Vinnie

CHAPTER TWO

Age 13

"Remind me why I have to go to this stupid dinner?" I complain to my nanny, Cecilia, as I look at her through the reflection of my vanity mirror.

Cecilia is less of a nanny and more of an older sister figure. She's twenty-three, and even though she was hired on to care for me, she and I quickly bonded, and the formalities dropped. Cecilia helps me with everything: school, hair, makeup, *boys*. She accompanies me to almost every event I am forced by my parents to attend. She even lives here at the estate, although her room isn't on the same floor as mine.

"Because, it's a charity fundraiser at the mayor's house and anyone worth a damn is invited," she reprimands as she lets a curl loose from the wand, letting the hot strand bounce against her hand as it immediately starts to cool.

She passes the handle of the curling wand to me so I can hold it while she sprays my hair with hairspray.

"The Townsends will be there," she continues with a coy smile. "I was talking to Esther today. She said Summer is ecstatic to go tonight."

I roll my eyes at the mention of Summer, and her keeper—I mean nanny—Esther.

Summer is three years younger than I am and tries desperately to act like she's my age. I only tolerate her presence at these dumb events because of her brother. Her brother makes my heart soar. I've had a crush on him since I was five.

I try to act casual as I ask Cecilia, "And Mason? Will he be there?"

She releases another curl and hands the wand back to me. Her lips turn up into a cheeky smile. "Maybe."

"Make sure my hair is perfect," I snap, but a smile plays against my lips as she narrows her eyes at me.

"I may be hired to be your nanny, young lady, but I'm still older than you. It'd behoove you to remember that."

"And it'd behoove *you* to remember that I'm your boss."

We stare at each other through the mirror for several seconds, our expressions hard, before we both burst into laughter.

She pokes my side with her freshly manicured fingernail. "You're a little princess, Vinnie. You're lucky I'm so fond of you."

"Mmmhmm," I hum and bring a tube of pink gloss to

my lips. Mom won't let me wear makeup yet, but she lets Cecilia style my hair however I want, and buys me a new lip gloss whenever I ask. This one tastes like cotton candy.

When my hair is done, I stand, and Cecilia grabs my dress from where it hangs nearby. It's beautiful. Ice-blue chiffon with a fitted bodice, and thick straps that tie on the top of my shoulders. It reminds me of a modern-day Cinderella, without the hoop skirt.

Shrugging from my robe, Cecilia slips the dress over my outstretched arms, careful as she brings it over my head, as to not ruin my hair or rub my gloss. Once I'm situated, she zips the back and turns me toward my mirror.

It's lovely. I can't wait for Mason to see me in it, and I wonder if he'll finally notice me as *more* than just a childhood playmate.

- - -

Mayor Conrad Moser's charity dinner is an absolute snoozefest. Nothing more than a four-course meal in their grand ballroom, packed with round tables for the most elite New York families to pretend like they care what each other has to say.

Mom insisted we attend tonight when Mayor Moser extended the invitation. This is their first social gathering in their new luxury 5th Avenue penthouse, since typically parties were thrown at their main residence, Gracie Mansion. Mom gushed about how close they live to the Met, if only part-time, and how she couldn't wait to see it because it was a tri-level penthouse—a unique rarity at this level of extravagance. So naturally, Father accepted the invitation, and here we are.

The auction was the most entertaining part of the evening, and even that was hardly bearable.

Leaning against my mother's shoulder, my finger traces along the extravagant beadwork on her tight champagne and gold gown. I was underdressed in comparison to her, but as she liked to remind me, "it's not your job to stand out, Vincenza."

Yet.

It's not my job to stand out, *yet*.

But I will, someday soon.

"Mom, can I go find the boys?" I ask, waiting until there is a lull in her conversation with Mayor Moser's wife, Elena. My brothers had slipped from the room ages ago and were probably exploring the grounds or playing with some of the other kids I saw earlier who have also disappeared. Who I really want to find, though, is Mason.

Looking around the ballroom, I realize I'm the only kid still sitting with their parents.

"Sure, sweetheart, but be careful wandering about on your own until you find them."

Smiling tightly, I stand and slightly bow my head as a sign of respect to Mrs. Moser. "Dinner was lovely. Thank you so much, Mrs. Moser."

"What a well-mannered daughter you have, Leighton," she praises. "A little not-so-well-kept secret, my dear. If you go through the main doors and up the staircase to the third floor, you'll find an access door to the roof. Somehow, all the children find a way to sneak into my rooftop hideaway. It's not much, but the view of the city is breathtaking."

"Thank you," I tell her, then spin on my heel and force every bone in my 'well-mannered' body to walk, *not run*, across the ballroom and to the stairs.

My nude sling-back kitten heels echo against the dark wooden staircase as I climb higher, craning my neck to see if anyone is on the second floor. It's quiet up here, so I turn immediately and climb the second staircase leading to the third floor.

Once at the top, I find the door Mrs. Moser mentioned will take me to the roof. For whatever reason though, I hesitate before stepping toward it.

My gaze sweeps over the ostentatious landing of the third floor and catches on a set of glass French doors that are slightly open. A light breeze ruffles the sheer curtains of the window next to it, the sounds of the bustling city pouring in.

I cross the space, drawn to the open doors, and push one just enough for me to slide through the gap.

Pressing my back against the door, it clicks into place, and the moment it does, a boy about my age slips out of the shadow cast by the wall of the balcony.

He wears simple black dress pants and a crisp white buttoned shirt, with a plain maroon tie hanging around his neck. But perhaps the most captivating thing this boy wears is his expression.

He looks sad, and angry, and above all, he looks lonely.

Something about his scowl makes me want to take his sadness away. I want to make him smile.

"Hi," I say shyly, tucking a lock of hair behind my ear.

"Hi," he replies, and takes a seat on the stone bench in the center of the balcony. From there, he stares straight out at the lights of the city.

"What are you doing up here?"

"Probably the same thing you are."

"Oh. Well, I was actually looking for my brothers."

"Haven't seen them," he says with boredom. It makes me deflate a little inside.

"Do you want company?" I ask as I take a step forward.

His head swings toward me, and he looks me up and down before turning back to the city. Nodding once, he says, "Sure, but can we not talk?"

"Okay."

Rounding the bench, I sit down next to him, leaving as much space between us as possible. I follow his line of sight and stare out at the twinkling skyscrapers. A few blocks over, a helicopter lands on the roof of Lenox Hill.

After several minutes, I can't take the silence. "Are you sitting up here alone because something made you sad?"

"I thought we agreed no talking."

My mouth opens, then closes again. There are so many questions on the tip of my tongue. A large part of me thinks it may be wise to go leave and find Mason, or my brothers, after all.

The boy exhales and leans forward with his elbows

pressed against his knees. "Sì," he sighs. "I miss my home. I wish to go back."

"I'm sure your family will be leaving soon. The auction has finished and everyone is just talking and dancing."

He laughs as I speak, turning to look at me. With his full attention, it feels like there is a spotlight shining down on me, the warmth of the light stifling. I squirm uncomfortably.

"I did not mean my house, I meant my *home*. Verona."

"As in Italy?"

"Sì. The one and only."

"Wow," I whisper to myself, before asking. "What's it like there? I've always dreamt of visiting. I'm half Italian, possibly a little more. My father is full, and my mother is half, mixed with Irish and French."

"It's very beautiful. A different beauty than New York has to offer." He looks back out to the skyline. His tone is a little more chipper when he eventually turns back to me. "Were you born here? You must have been—your accent is purely American."

"I was. Right here in New York, actually. My mom was born in Virginia and happened to meet my father when he was here for a summer abroad. They fell in love and he moved to the U.S. for her, and they settled here." It's more information than a teenage boy needs, but I love the story of my parents. Their love story gives me hope I'll find my own someday. If they could find their soulmate by chance, after living an ocean apart for so long, certainly destiny has plans for all of us.

"Romantic," he says, scrunching his nose slightly, though his voice holds no sarcasm.

"When did you move her—"

"Vincenza!" My mom stops my sentence, her voice carrying through the closed doors as she looks for me.

His gaze snaps back to mine when he hears my mom, and I swear I see his eyes widen for a moment.

I sigh with annoyance. I want to know more about this boy...hear more about growing up in Italy, and why he's here. How long he's lived here. But instead, I discreetly wipe my sweaty palms on the underside of my dress and stand.

"I have to go. Thank you for keeping me company." Smiling sweetly, I notice the way he stares blankly at me instead of returning the sentiment. It wipes the smile off my face, and I take steps backward to the door, not taking my eyes off him as he continues to stare at me with a cold look in his.

He glares at me as I twist the handle and step back into the penthouse, wondering where I went wrong.

Boys are so confusing.

"Oh, there you are, sweetheart! I was worried when your brothers showed back up at the table, but you weren't with them. It's time to go—your father's already sent for the car."

"Alright." I follow her to the staircase, and grab onto the railing, turning to glance over my shoulder one more time at where the boy sits alone again, cloaked in the night's darkness. I can just make out his silhouette, and I ignore my inner persuasion that begs for me to go back out there and find out what I did to offend him.

Back on the main floor of the penthouse, Mayor Moser's coat check attendant drapes my black coat over my shoulders. My father and brothers position their own coats, adjusting them while they talk amongst themselves.

When my mother ushers me into the waiting elevator and asks me if I had fun this evening, it's with the *ding* of the doors enclosing our family inside that I realize I never even got the boy's name.